Escaping the Chaos

Reuniting the States

Gregory B Grinstead

Copyright

Escaping the Chaos
Reuniting the States

First Printing December 2019

Books > Christian > Politics
Books > Capitalism > Politics
Books > Democracy > Socialism

ISBN: 9781675140826

Contents

Dedications

This book is dedicated to my wife
Michelle

She stands by my side
As we fight the good fight.

We hold these truths to be self-evident, that all men are created equal, that they are endowed by their Creator with certain unalienable Rights, that among these are Life, Liberty and the pursuit of Happiness.
Excerpt from Declaration of Independence

We the People of the United States, in Order to form a more perfect Union, establish Justice, insure domestic Tranquility, provide for the common defense, promote the general Welfare, and secure the Blessings of Liberty to ourselves and our Posterity, do ordain and establish this Constitution for the United States of America.
The Preamble to the Constitution

1

The Right to Pay – ARM 2

I would like $2232.00 please." The man was holding a gun and had a mask over his face.

The clerk seemed to not be concerned with the gun or the bright orange mask and counted out $2232.00 and gave it to him.

The man walked out of the First Bank of Newton and jumped into the waiting car. As they quickly drove away, the man with the mask looked at the driver and said, "Make sure that you count it and initial it, so I don't get a fine from the auditors, like last week."

"Where's the next stop?"

As they drove to the next bank, to make another unauthorized withdrawal, they drove by a large billboard.

FINANCIAL HELP IS A RIGHT OF EVERY CITIZEN

Dennis Flanders – everyone calls him Denny – is using the same Tag Line he used 6 years ago. And why not? It had gotten him elected to one of the 3 top positions of the *1st Quarter's* Administration.

A majority of voters had agreed with Denny. When someone does not have enough money to pay their bills, how can anyone deny them the money they need to live a normal life. It was Denny's hard work on the *Right to Pay Initiative* 6 years ago that sealed his position of leadership in the *1st Quarter's* Administration.

It was the details of how to get the needed money to the right families under the *Right to Pay Initiative* that had brought four distinct groups into one united front against poverty. The four groups now sponsored political candidates under one name – The United Battle Against Poverty - UBAP. The UBAP candidates had been on a long winning streak since the *Right to Pay Initiative* had been started by the three Administrators.

After 4 more stops, the two men were done for the day, with no problems from local Law Enforcement. James had been restricted to driving because he had made several serious errors of judgment in the past as the trigger man. Financial Counselors Inc. (FCI), his employer could no longer trust him to collect the unauthorized withdrawals.

It was James's job to drive and count the money that the Masked Man collected. Getting these unauthorized withdrawals was the process of obtaining actual dollars to keep the *Right to Pay Initiative* funded.

James's errors of judgment, as the Masked Man had almost taken the life of a bank teller and guard, even though they had recognized the bright orange mask he was wearing. The guard was young and made several quick movements and without thinking, James shot past the teller's head and then turned and blew out the front window of the newly opened *Bank of New POP1*. FCI immediately demoted him to Driver. They let him keep his gun.

James and his masked passenger returned to their employer early.

"So, James, everything go, OK?" The man sitting at the desk, next to the rollup door was looking intently at a series of monitors and not at James. "Why so early?"

James's partner answered, "Charter Bank, on South Street has closed. The sign was still up, but the doors were locked, and the lights were out."

As the roll-up door closed, the man behind the desk looked up from the monitors, "The second closure this month - I had nothing on my App about this."

James gave the man the orange zippered bag containing $27,386 from the day's six unauthorized withdrawals. James used to call them "robberies" but was taught the proper wording in his New Morality Training Classes. The amounts from each location were written and neatly initialed by him and the masked man on the FCI paper form inside the orange bag.

As the masked man walked to the door leading outside, he turned and said to no one in particular, "The Administration is going to have to do something about the closures. These greedy banks continue to try to stop the unauthorized withdrawals, just on the principle of the thing. They have plenty of money. Why do they care if a few poor people can pay their bills?"

2

The Right to Pay - ARM 1

T he *Right to Pay Initiative* had three separate and distinct processing agencies or ARMS. Each ARM had gone into effect gradually, giving the *1st Quarter* Administration time to educate everyone on the moral correctness of the *Right to Pay Initiative.*

The *4th Quarter*, never to be outdone by the *1st Quarter*, had also adopted the three ARMS of the *Right to Pay Initiative* 4 years ago. For 4 years both the *1st Quarter* and *4th Quarter* had been working hard educating everyone on the benefits of the program.

Jerry sat with his girlfriend, in the neat outer office of Financial Counselors Incorporated. FCI's sign was made of poster board in the window behind them.

FINANCIAL COUNSELORS INC.
When you can't afford to pay, we can help
A Right to Pay Company

The older woman behind the desk seemed very concerned. FCI picked their screeners carefully. Each screener brought the motherly characteristic of a deeply caring counselor. They were sitting in a simple office in the lower-rent section of New POP1.

Jerry and Ana had come to this Northern Branch because of its low profile. Last year there had been very loud and public demonstrations at the larger FCI branches. Now ARM 1 used temporary sites and moved every 3 months.

The older woman asked again, "How much do you need to pay your bills?" Jerry and Ana really didn't know how much money they needed, and it was the job of the screener to find out. Of course, the screener never called herself a screener. She was a Financial Counselor. And she was there to help.

Just behind her desk and above her head was a very professional portrait of her smiling a sympathetic smile. Under the portrait was an Official Plaque - **Financial Counselor.** In smaller letters under the Plaque was an official seal that stated **ARM 1 – The Right to Pay Initiative.**

Jerry looked sheepishly at the motherly woman. "Our families don't like us coming here. They are afraid that our names will be registered. Don't get me wrong. They believe in the New Morality."

The woman smiled, "Our kind leaders of the *1st Quarter* understand the stigma that can come with asking for help. They have given FCI instructions to not keep any records after 90 days. That way, we track your financial progress over a three-month period and then your records are shredded. You don't have to worry about the greed of the ignorant ones out there. They may protest but the Law is the Law."

After filling out the paper form with information about their rent, utilities, credit card payments and misc. debts, they were told they needed an extra $6332 to pay their the next 3 months bills. The woman made calculations and finalized the transaction with a request.

"Would you like to join the *1st Quarter's* voters block, The United Battle Against Poverty – UBAP?" I see here that you are new to the *1st Quarter*. But we don't discriminate against newcomers."

Jerry and Ana became members of UBAP that day. Next election they would vote for Denny – for sure. Jerry thought, "How could political groups exist that don't want to fight poverty?"

3

The Right to Pay – ARM 3

The fight is a clear fight. It is not hard to understand… that when people don't have enough money… to pay their bills in our rich nation, something is wrong. And we are… fixing the problem. Our enemies are easily identified…"

Denny Flanders was making a rare appearance at one of the *1st Quarter's* Media Centers. This Media Center had been given the job of educating everyone on the moral correctness of the *Right to Pay Initiative.* ARM 3 of the program. Standing on a sturdy desk Denny talked fast but paused every few words. Two men had helped him up onto the desk so all the media cubical stations could see and hear him.

This room had 120 media stations creating and monitoring the educational stories of the *1st Quarter* Administration's great success with the *Right to Pay Initiative.* ARM3 had an undisclosed budget since it was determined that budgetary accountability would have a chilling effect upon educators. And no one wanted to appear to be against education. No one had asked how a room full of media storytellers were classified as educators.

Denny continued with his staccato sentences and uneven pauses. "Those who oppose us… are either greedy or worse. The rich of this mighty… nation have for too long… kept the money for themselves. They are right now… sponsoring our greedy enemies. But… if we keep our eyes on the prize, we can defeat them… once and for all. You can win by educating our citizens. You can win."

Everyone in the room was keenly focused upon Denny's frail body as it rocked back and forth. Many were wondering if he was going to fall off the desk and if anyone would catch him. Some of these storytellers were already writing the Headline.

Denny Flanders injured by Anti - *Right to Pay Initiative* protesters at ARM3 Educational Center

Before Denny Flanders could fall, giving many in the room the chance to out-do themselves with stories, two men helped Denny off the desk. Denny left the room with two other men following close behind him.

Denny and the other 2 Administrators of the *1st Quarter* had not come today to give a pep-talk. They had come to go over the biannual figures of the *Right to Pay Initiative* ARM1, ARM2 and ARM3.

Since ARM3 was the media - educational side of the legislation, the numbers were irrelevant. But the three Top Administrators would still meet with ARM3's leadership team.

Denny entered the large adjoining room with Gordon and Raul (pronounced Ra-U-all). Each took their place on the three chairs on the platform in the front. Sitting on each side of them, on one level down were their trusted staff members. This room had a platform that was three-tiered and specifically designed by the Top Administrators.

The design of all the meetings that the Top Administrators attended had been guided by an unspoken political axiom. ***Appearance is more important than reality.*** The level a person was sitting on aligned with their present position of power and compensation. The Administration's employee's ambition was to move up in the room, not to do their jobs well.

As ARM3's Media leadership team filed into the room, they looked up to see three men sitting on the highest level, with two staff members sitting one level down. The two staff members faced out toward the attendees. They saw three sets of three watching them intently.

Denny was in the center. Gordon and his staff members were on the right and Raul and his staff members on his left. This meeting room had been designed to be the opposite of a round table discussion.

The Media Center leadership team sat in one row of chairs facing the platform. Each senior leader had four junior leaders sitting behind them. The senior leaders' faces looked as if they were sitting in the front row of a firing squad.

Denny's staff member spoke first. There were no greetings or niceties as had just been expressed in the Media Room. "Jim, what did you think was going to happen if you shut down those demonstrations at Charter Bank?"

"Here in Richmond, no one wants to demonstrate. Our salaries depend upon the success of the *1st Quarter's* Administration. But in Newton and the cities close to the *2nd Quarter's* border, people want to demonstrate."

Jim sitting just off-center, in the front row, tried to respond. "It looked like things were getting out of..."

Immediately Gordon's main staffer interrupted. "It makes people feel good to demonstrate. It makes them feel like they are doing something to right a wrong. As long as you control the Media coverage with your educational programs, don't shut the Anti-*Right to Pay Initiative's* protestors down. Let them make a lot of noise and then re-label them through your media educational stories."

Denny cleared his throat and a hush fell on the room. "What we need is... a correct naming of those who... are against the poor and... against solving poverty... once and for all. Maybe your creative minds can come up with something better... But why don't we start calling the demonstrators *The Greedy Crowd*?"

Gordon waited respectfully, thinking that Denny's pauses had something to do with his brain catching up to his mouth. When it looked like Denny was done, Gordon spoke up, "*Greed* is a great way to define our opponents. I agree with Denny."

Raul thought to himself, "Everyone's definition of greed is different, but everyone is against it."

Raul's main aid, Jovana spoke to a woman sitting next to Jim, "Joyce, begin to incorporate in all your educational materials the term *Greedy Crowd.*"

Raul, sitting on the left, spoke up, "Joyce, don't even audience test this. Denny has a keen sense of what is happening in the minds of our followers at UBAP. Just get the word out, that those who oppose us are just an unruly greedy mob of people who are not concerned with the poor. Let Richards try to fight that image for a while."

Jim seemed to relax slightly as the focus was directed at something other than his using the local Law Enforcement to shut down three protests on the same day at three separate Charter Bank locations. But Gordon's staff member brought the subject back to Jim.

"Jim, you can either get your act together or find another job outside of Richmond. It looks like Charter may be pulling out of the *1ˢᵗ Quarter* since they were never on board with us like the 3 Big Banks. Now we have more people angry in Newton and the surrounding cities."

Raul spoke up, "Jim, are you that dull. Can't you remember the main rule of the unwritten rules of Media Centers? *If you think something is getting out of hand, call our friends at The Morality Warriors.* But don't publicly call them our "friends." We are not affiliated with their methods and are not responsible for what they do. Just call them."

Jim wanted to get the focus onto someone other than himself. "When Franklin called the Morality Warriors last year, for the Old Augusta protests, three people died."

Raul cut Jim off, "And the rioters were dispersed and the Anti- *Right to Pay Initiative* demonstrators were blamed for everything that happened. Get it? Let them riot just a little. Then if it escalates call in the Morality Warriors. Then use YOUR Media Center to rewrite the story. Damn Jim, you are so slow."

Looking to the man sitting further down the row from Jim, Raul smiled and said, "Good job Franklin. You were right calling in the Morality Warriors. Even if people got hurt."

Another of Denny's staff members opened a large notebook and began to address each person sitting in front of her and slightly below her, one at a time.

"Frank - let's start with you. How is the campaign to discredit all local financial institutions who are not actively supporting us?"

The meeting continued with occasional interjections from the Top 3 Administrators. Most of the details were handled by their staff.

One man stood at the back of the room off to the right side watching intently. His name was Erick Swan and he was recording everything for his employer DRAG Systems.

Erick Swan was a shadowy character who had learned to blend into every type of crowd. Now he stood silently, and thought to himself, "These idiots really believe what they say. They make a declaration, and then it is true. No matter how stupid."

4

The New Morality Training

James drove the 90 minutes to his condo in New POP1 and dropped his rental car off.

FCI drivers were not allowed to work in the cities they lived in. James went directly home. A few years ago, he would have stayed and talked with whoever would listen. But since he had married Janet, he enjoyed coming home.

James was slow. He had been in the *Special Classes* in High School. But James had three valuable qualities - loyalty, integrity and he would always try to get the job done, even when he had no idea how to do it. FCI was looking for a few good people who could accomplish ARM2 of the *Right to Pay Initiative* and James needed a job.

Janet greeted James as he walked into their Condo on the 5th floor of the older 20 story building in New POP1. James had one other quality that only a few close friends knew about. He could remember numbers and series of numbers. Each day James would give his wife the exact amount that FCI collected in unauthorized withdrawals from the banks he visited.

Now Janet sat with James and made out a fake shopping list. Janet wrote the number of the day of the week and the number of the week in the month on the top of the list.

Then she wrote her shopping list that corresponded to that day's *Right to Pay* collections - $27,386.

2 gallons of milk   8 small spice packets
7 cans of corn   6 lbs. of hamburger
3 loaves - wheat bread

The New Morality Training

James had been introduced to Janet by Tom. No one knew Tom's last name. It changed depending upon the group he was in. Tom had been a Believers Lay-Pastor. Believers were not allowed to meet in the *1st Quarter*. The Believers leaders never used their last names for security reasons.

Tom had attended James's wedding in the official New Morality Service and had also officiated at his Believers wedding. James and Janet were a part of the underground Believers group that Tom led in New POP1. They would meet as a yoga exercise group, on Thursdays at 5 p. m. Janet gave Tom the FCI Collection figures every week at the Believers meeting.

Tom and the Believers had helped James when it looked like he was going to be terminated from FCI. When James had accidentally shot at a bank teller and guard, he broke down emotionally. The help he received with his daily life pressures had been the reason James had become a Believer.

With long talks, prayer, and belief in the Book, James had overcome the problems a guy from the *Special Classes* faced. Tom had encouraged James to stay at FCI. Tom, Janet, and James had a mission and having James on the inside of ARM2 was helping the underground immensely.

The Believers did not agree with the New Morality. James was living a double life that challenged him daily. Janet and he would talk about the future when their mission would be over, and they could move to the *2nd Quarter* and be free.

Janet accompanied James that night to the final mandated class at the New Morality Service Building. FCI was required by the *1st Quarter* Administration to send any employees that did not exhibit the 2 *Commands of Love*, for more training in the New Morality. Shooting at an unarmed guard qualified as the need for more training.

The New Morality classes started with Sexual Tolerance and Male Sensitivity Training. James had breezed through these classes since he had been trained since High School that men should never exhibit *The Caveman Emotions*. Most important, he had been taught the 2 *Commands of Love*.

#1.
Loving People means promoting
Sexual Freedom and Tolerance
toward all Sexual Behaviors.

#2.
Loving People means promoting
Financial Justice and Equality
for all men in every circumstance.

These 2 *Commands of Love* were the foundation of the New Morality. James had to convince the teachers of this mandated class that he could do more than just repeat the 2 *Commands of Love*. He had to apply them to real-life problems and specific situations.

Janet was allowed to accompany James to the classes since he had been in the *Special Classes*. She would help him pass these final exams by being there as moral support. Tom had also asked Janet to guard James's responses if the Believers doctrines were in any of the exam questions.

As they drove into the large, lighted parking lot they saw the New Morality steeple on the bright new building's peak. The four-story building was set apart from other buildings of New POP1 by how many high-powered lights lighted the crystal and glass structure.

Two young friendly greeters welcomed Janet and James and directed them to their government-mandated class. They both gave their credit accounts, to the person behind the counter at the back of the class. The

1st *Quarter* Administration kept no records of marriage, so Janet had to pay separately from her husband.

The 1st *Quarter* was not against marriage. They actually encouraged men, women, and groups to get married as many times as they wanted. The 2 *Commands of Love* mandated an open attitude toward all.

As Janet walked into the classroom, she was surprised to see how many other people had brought emotional support. There were dogs, cats, and one ferret. She put her hand on James's arm and smiled to reassure him that all was well.

Behind the teacher, at the front of the class were the 2 *Commands of Love* and then a list of the 6 Principles of Behavior. The 1st *Quarter* Administration had been using these 6 Principles of Behavior to mandate new rules for all citizens.

6 PRINCIPLES OF BEHAVIOR

1. I will speak and act in accordance with the 2 *Commands of Love*.

2. I will report all my financial transactions to DRAG Systems.

3. I am not free to speak if my words offend a fellow citizen.

4. I will be sensitive to minor requests of fellow citizens and act accordingly.

5. I will use whatever means necessary to stop those around me from breaking the 2 *Commands of Love*.

6. My Independent Freedom should never supersede Community Freedom.

Janet was relieved as they drove home. James had passed with only a few errors of judgment. He had missed Question 6.

QUESTION 6

You see a person in his front yard talking to his neighbor about becoming a Believer and repeating the false wisdom of the Book. What do you do?

A. You talk with them about the 2 *Commands of Love* and the 6 Principles of Behavior.
B. You report this incident to DRAG Systems.
C. You identify yourself as a Morality Warrior and physically stop the conversation with whatever means necessary.

The correct answer was "C" from Rule 5. The correct answer was on the wall at the front of the classroom, but James was confused. He felt there was no wrong answer to this question, only a correct answer, and one less-correct answer. He was passed due to special considerations.

James had answered "B" because that would not require him to confront this neighbor. (James liked his neighbor and had taken the question literally.) The teacher explained to James that DRAG Systems did not want any information, except financial information.

The teacher then took the opportunity as a teaching moment for the whole class. "Can anyone tell me why James is wrong in answering Question 6 with "B" reporting this incident to DRAG Systems?"

No one spoke up since the mandatory attendees had learned over the last few weeks that being invisible was the best practice. Even if you had the right answer, most interchanges were designed to embarrass, bully or shut down any opinion other than the teacher's opinion.

The teacher continued, "DRAG Systems is very important. The *1st Quarter* could not create financial equality among citizens without the help of DRAG Systems. DRAG Systems tracks all financial transactions and uses that information to create equity among each trade and skill. If citizens report non-financial incidents, DRAG Systems would be slowed as it processes data."

The teacher patted James on the shoulder as James and Janet walked out of the classroom asking, "Would you like to join UBAP? The four groups that have formed for the *United Battle Against Poverty* are working closely with DRAG Systems."

Janet answered for James, "We joined last month." The Believers group had found that the names of people joining UBAP did not appear in the system for up to 6 weeks. This was the safest answer since no one could check. Of course, it was a lie.

It was harder and harder to avoid joining UBAP. Each supermarket now had *STAMP OUT POVERTY* campaigns, that they had decided to promote after a UBAP representative had explained the benefits of *The Right to Pay Initiative*. Everyone would have enough money to buy their products since the *Right to Pay Initiative* was giving help to the less fortunate. To most merchants, it looked like a Win/Win proposal.

The *STAMP OUT POVERTY* programs were voluntary and masqueraded as charity, but in all cases, UBAP promoted membership in their group as an option. You could not shop in most stores, without being approached by a "volunteer" asking the same question.

"Would you like to join UBAP?"

5

Relocating Charter Bank

How could this happen? 38% of our revenue comes from *1ˢᵗ Quarter* branches." Jerry was the Vice President in charge of expansion at Charter Bank. A decision had been made to no longer have branches in the *1ˢᵗ Quarter*. Jerry raised his voice, "This is the opposite of expansion!"

Tom (James and Janet's Lay-pastor) was a senior advisor to Charter Bank. He responded to Jerry, "In a few months the *Right to Pay Initiative* will lose its ability to rob from the 3 Big Banks and all smaller independent banks will be hit over and over again until we have no more assets in the *1ˢᵗ Quarter* anyway. My inside data shows a giant increase in needed funds. Where do you think Denny Flanders's Administration is going to get these ever-increasing amounts of money?"

The meeting was being held in a small room in the *3ʳᵈ Quarter*. Four Charter Bank Vice Presidents were meeting to discuss the complications of disconnecting from the *1ˢᵗ Quarter* without losing half their assets to DRAG System's fees and penalties.

Todd Edwards was in charge of shutting down his Division's remaining 15 banks, in the *1ˢᵗ Quarter*. He responded to Jerry, "I told you guys to either get all the way on board with the *Right to Pay Initiative* or we would be targeted disproportionally by FCI."

"Todd was right," interjected Tom. "I am not sure we should morally become a part of the official *Robin Hood* programs of the *1ˢᵗ Quarter*. But now it is too late, anyway. With the attacks of the Morality Warriors on 5 branches and FCI hitting us in 4 other cities, we will lose all our local business and start paying out funds that belong to the investors of the *2ⁿᵈ Quarter* in less than four months."

Tom looked at Rick Sosa, the man over the *2nd Quarter's* 23 locations, and continued, "Rick, Jerry and Todd – if you work together, we might actually profit from this action. I have data from FCI's Northern unauthorized withdrawals – I mean robberies.

"The problems of the *Right to Pay Initiative* are much greater than anyone had anticipated. By growing business accounts in the *2nd Quarter* and registering to do business in the *3rd Quarter*, we may be ahead of the other smaller banks."

Todd Edwards's attitude perked up. He was always ready for a challenge and most would say he was a man's man (but not in the New Morality classes - of course). "OK, I will work with Jerry and his expansion team to bring all our *1st Quarter* locations to the *3rd Quarter*. We will close and relocate managers and key employees to the *3rd Quarter* if they want to move west. I wouldn't mind living here in the *3rd Quarter* too."

The financial growth numbers for the Middle Quarters were not available for the Charter Bank executives or any other bank's executives to use for new growth projects. The middle Quarters had instituted privacy rules over all business transactions when DRAG Systems tried to install their data-gathering devices.

In the *1st Quarter* and the *4th Quarter* regional data could be bought from unofficial DRAG Systems' employees by businesses trying to gain an edge over their competition. But the Middle Quarters had stopped DRAG Systems from operating in the middle of the country.

Tom continued talking through the plan. "We might not have the numbers of the middle of the country's financial condition but look around. Every city I visit has large building programs. You all know what the east coast looks like."

Tom closed the meeting with, "OK, Charter Bank is moving all its business from the *1st Quarter* to the *3rd Quarter*. I will inform the appropriate corporate departments through hard copies only. I am driving West. When you guys fly back to the east coast, don't mention you have seen me.

Tom – was driving to an important meeting with the Believers and two other Freedom Groups in the *3rd Quarter*.

6

The Believers Unite to Fight

The house was set back off the road. The gate, intercom, and pole with the solar array was the only publicly visible acknowledgment that there was someone's residence up the gravel road running off this back highway.

The leaders of the Believers were meeting in this house. 24 men and women had come in 8 cars this morning to meet with the Ex-Californian who had lived here for the last 12 years. He had escaped California 3 years before the Big One – as the 9 point earthquake is now called. He had sold his businesses 2 years before DRAG Systems started monitoring all *4th Quarter* business assets and transactions.

Light snow had fallen the night before, and those from the South were nervously wondering if they were going to get snowed-in on this 20-acre property several miles out of Iowa's largest city.

"Does the city grade that road out there?" The South Coast Believers' Representative wondered out loud.

The Ex-Californian was being a good host. "Don't worry. We are set up to weather any storm. Let's sit in the Great Room and talk. Here are the guidelines for our meeting to avoid confusion."

1. We are free to express our own opinions without fear.
2. We will respect one another's personal perspective.
3. We are free to cooperate or not cooperate as we see fit.

The Ex-Californian stood up to address the group. They were casually scattered around the Great Room of his house. "Welcome to my home. I have only one request of my fellow leaders of Believer Groups and then I will turn this meeting over to Tom.

"I would like to encourage each of us to use our secular talents to serve our communities outside of our Believer Groups. The old ways are in the past, and we need to be involved with the people who need us the most. Most of the people who need our spiritual help are in the secular businesses and other organizations of our communities.

"Don't wait for our communities to fall prey to the deceptions of DRAG Systems and the ridiculous ideas of the New Morality. I know you want to influence. So, let us influence from relationships we develop outside our Believer Groups. That is enough of my preaching.

"Now I would like to turn this meeting over to Tom. He has reported some interesting developments and then Chris from the northern 4th Quarter also has some news."

Tom had driven 10 hours from the Charter Bank Corporate meetings two days before. He stood up, "We are meeting close to the geographic center of our country and I think that is significant.

"The 1st Quarter is losing capital and businesses at an ever-increasing rate. I am not sure what will happen once DRAG Systems recognizes that the financial condition of their two participating Quarters is unsustainable. But if I had to guess, DRAG Systems will be coming after the middle of the country's financial systems and the liberty we presently enjoy.

"We have several strategies in place to help the weaker businesses who are being hurt the most by the Right to Pay Initiative. Pray that we will be successful."

The Believers Unite to Fight

Chris from *4th Quarter*-North stood as Tom sat down. "I would like to ask everyone here who lives in the Free *Quarters* to consider finding and commissioning men and women who can do the following."

Chris handed out one sheet of paper that he had put a lot of thought into. "Let us all try to find and support these…" He read off the paper.

1. People who can and will articulate why freedom helps **everyone** – especially the poor.

2. People who can and will articulate the Book's emphasis on Personal Ownership of Property.

3. Find men and women who will have the courage to talk publicly, even when attacked.

4. Find men and women who will talk about these subjects in all the Believers Groups, so Believers will stand against the anticipated DRAG Systems' deceptions.

5. Find men and women who will talk about courage among all our Believers Groups and how wisdom and courage should be emphasized as the qualities that are needed, as we resist the totalitarian takeover of our communities."

Chris was a father of 4 girls. He was in his forties but looked like he was 30 years old. He looked as if he was about to break down, "If we had done these 5 things - 12 years ago, we may have the freedom to live as Believers, now in the *4th Quarter*. But we were asleep. We thought that the freedom we enjoyed up north would be there for our…" Chris became overwhelmed with emotion and stopped.

A Representative from a South Liberty Group that had lived most of his life in the *2nd Quarter* spoke. "It is the Government Officials that we have to convince to be courageous. They are so cowardly. Most of our politicians are people pleasers and not fighters. You can get a long way in politics being a people pleaser, BUT you cannot win a fight that you don't fight."

An older woman in the back asked, "How do we promote fighters to run for the regional government offices? If the passive, unprincipled men and women are elected, how can we stop them?"

The Ex-California answered, "We have to do 2 things.

"1 – Teach Believers that fighting is good and NOT bad when you are fighting for the right things.

"2 – Find men who are willing to fight and sacrifice for the right principles.

"The other side has men and women who do this, and their principles are immoral and evil. We MUST find those who can and will FIGHT."

The meeting continued as each Believer spoke about specific problems in their regions. The discussions continued through dinner – which is called supper in the *3rd Quarter*. The group continued to talk informally at breakfast the next morning.

As breakfast was winding down, the Ex-California stood and thanked each Believer for coming and had a final request. "As you all go back to where God has you, please reach out to the Believer Groups that don't talk with you.

"If we do not stop fighting with EACH other about the small differences in our doctrines, we will never win the real battle for our freedoms. Some of your fellow Believers have already been deceived and think DRAG Systems is great since they don't understand DRAG Systems' Mission Statement. They have tunnel vision. You may not be able to break the deception, but we can stop dividing into ineffectual camps."

Something unusual began to happen among the group. As the Liberty Group leaders watched, several people began to talk about how they had caused hurt and division in their areas among the other Believers

Groups. Sincere disagreements had turned into behind the scenes gossip sessions. These disagreements led to distorting the other's ideas to get people on their side. Jealousy, envy, anger, and hurts had closed their hearts to the people who they were supposed to work with.

A simple prayer ended the meeting.

May God help us to do EPH3-4 – For the good of the Resistance.

May God help us FIGHT.

May God help us work hard to establish Justice and Righteousness in every area of our communities.

Amen.

7

The Liberty Groups Are Exposed

Tom drove 3 hours south from the Believers' strategy meeting to the Intermodal Inland Port in the center of the country to meet two separate Liberty Groups, who could not attend the Iowa meeting.

Tom decided that he would not meet next to the 4 Federal Facilities next to the Intermodal. Instead, he would meet in a city that had refused to change its name in the Purity Purges 12 years ago. Independence was scheduled to be renamed 3POP-18 and those living in Old Missouri resisted the Federal *Offensive Name Act.*

Missouri's rebellion sparked a push back to the Purity Purges and although Richmond's documents all have 3POP-18 on the official map of the country, the *3rd Quarter* refused to change any names.

The *2nd Quarter* then followed their example and changed all names back to the original names. The *Offensive Name Act* was enacted for all names that someone found offensive. After one year of hearings, it was decided that most names were offensive, and the numeric naming of all communities was forced upon the Nation. But one half the country refused to go along with the mandates. The push back on renaming of cities split the 2nd and 3rd Quarter Administrations from the east and west coast Administrations.

Tom arrived in KC and prepared to meet with the two Southern Liberty Groups. They had sent representatives to discuss coordinating their political actions with the Believers Groups. These two groups, the Citizens for Independence and the Liberty Coalition had 50% Believers and 50% rebellious men who wanted to be free. They had sent 2 people from each of their regions. Tom was to act as an outsider and find how the groups could coordinate their actions.

The Liberty Groups Are Exposed

Tom sat in the back of the church as he waited for the representatives to show up. He held slips of paper with a café's address in Independence Missouri where they were to meet later that day. Each representative walked in and sat with the person they had come with. The last person, who Tom knew was from the Citizens for Independence, 2nd Quarter - South was accompanied by a stranger – Erick Swan.

Tom had one rule for all his meetings. He had to know and have a history with each person. Tom quietly walked out of the side door of the building throwing the slips of paper in the exterior trash.

He would have to contact the Citizens for Independence and question why they had sent a person he did not know. He would also inform the other groups that their identities may have been compromised.

Tom drove East to Springfield Illinois to meet with the Northern Liberty Groups. Springfield was on the Northern Border of the 2nd Quarter. He would make sure that in this meeting only men and women who had been vetted would attend.

Old Springfield IL– 2POP4

Tom took more precautions when he arrived in Springfield. It was a border city. Some of the most radical Morality Warriors were based in the regions North of Springfield, called the *Lawless Lands*.

When the Federal Government finally lost legitimacy the Northern regions of Illinois broke and became a No-State area. The Federal authorities were sometimes recognized and other times the 2nd Quarter Authorities were recognized. But most of the time the area was ruled by the person with the biggest gun. There was no local Law Enforcement.

"What happened in KC? I thought you were meeting with us." The man sitting with Tom had worked with him a decade earlier at Charter Bank.

Tom responded, "There was a stranger with the Southern Representative for the Citizens for Independence. I will not meet with someone that has not been vetted. He was a stranger to me."

Tom's friend explained, "The story is that the Rep. that was supposed to come to KC was in a car wreck last week. He sent a replacement, that has been very active in the South. This guy is a good guy and they have known him since the Missouri push back."

Tom responded, "I took a picture of him in KC and I will go to Richmond and see if I can try to find out more on him. Try to get me his full name and any other personal info you might have." Tom knew his friend would try hard to investigate this further.

"Let's meet tomorrow. Ask each person to bring any information on their friendly contacts in banks or other businesses in their areas. My goal is to develop current data on *The Right to Pay Initiative's* unauthorized withdrawals.

"The *1ˢᵗ Quarter* is bleeding capital as more and more investors refuse to subsidize the poor with no accountability or records of the program's finances. I think they are also getting very tired of every transaction being watched by DRAG Systems.

Tom ended the meeting with, "Get our friends together tomorrow at the last place we met. After the meeting, I will go to Richmond as soon as I can."

8

Free Men Push Back

Janet sat with James. "OK, let's go over it again. Tomorrow, instead of total numbers, bring me each entry in the book. Also, I need what Bank or Credit Union you steal money from." Janet refused to use the deceptive wording of the *1ˢᵗ Quarter* Administration. Janet hated confusion.

Tom wanted to collect more information from the New POP1 areas for the Liberty Groups and their bank and business contacts in the Middle *Quarters*. Janet would gather the numbers from each unauthorized withdrawal from James and report to Tom.

As James left to take the train to the FCI warehouse area, he looked perplexed. Janet rested her hand upon his hand and assured him that if he got the bank's names mixed up that was OK. "Just do your best and keep the numbers coming."

James parked his rental car inside the warehouse and walked to the air-conditioned staging area. The windows had been boarded up years ago and the door was oversized metal with a small window. He looked at the cameras above his head and smiled. He was happy to be back doing something productive.

"James, you and your partner need to complete your review training today, before you go out. Take room three, he is already in there – just start the video." The man at the makeshift counter gestured to his right down the dark hallway, without looking up.

James greeted his partner with a daily greeting he had observed others doing. His partner looked up nodded and hit the play button on the small screen before them.

"Hello and welcome to your Review Training. This bi-annual training is given so you can succeed in your very important job." James's partner grunted. James followed his lead and grunted too.

The man on the screen had a large **RIGHT TO PAY** sign painted on the wall behind him. He looked very official. James tried to concentrate on what he was saying "... remember ... never tell anyone what you do, where you go, what you take as an unauthorized collector for our very important program. ARM2 – collections are imperative to the success of providing equity to our community."

James looked confused, "Imperative?" but the man was continuing. "There are some who because of a "lack of love" do not want us to do our jobs. They are greedy and usually have a lot of money themselves and they don't want to share."

The video droned on and on and James's mind wondered. James thought his partner might have fallen asleep. The video finally ended. The two men signed a form laying on the table by the door and started the day later than normal.

James and his orange masked friend's day went uneventful for the first two stops. Their third stop was not routine.

The orange masked man jumped into James's car out of breath. "Get out of here, NOW."

James looked at him.

"Drive, Now!" The man shouted again, this time with panic in his voice.

James sped away, with his mind not reacting as fast as his body. James made a quick right and scrapped the side of a pole on the right. Then a quick left and scrapped a car on his left. The masked man looked at James, now with fear of James's driving. James's emergency driving skills were being revealed for the first time.

"OK - Slow down a little bit." James's passenger said in a calmer voice. He was watching James closely.

James kept his eyes on the street ahead and didn't slow down. "What happened?"

"SLOW down NOW." James slammed on the breaks and it was now evident to the masked man sitting next to him that he may have to drive. James's mind did not process information at a speed needed in an emergency.

"OK pull into the alley up to your right, slowly. See there - Slowly." The masked man took a deep breath. "James, just breathe!"

James again said, "What happened?" Now that the car was stopped, and the parking brake was on.

The orange masked partner started, "Everything was going as it always does. Then the teller looked to her right and dropped to the floor. I saw a man with a White Mask over his face and then I heard the shot as I saw his gun. He shot over my head and I shot back. I think he had on body armor. I might have hit him, but he just looked at me and shot over my head again.

"Then he said to me that I had 5 seconds to leave or I would be dead.
"I left...
"I'm done...
"I quit...
"Take me back to my car."

James looked at him, still not fully understanding. But now he understood that he would also be in trouble for not finishing the route of the day if he took him to his car. Slowly James decided to drive to the next collection area.

James slowly said, "I will go in and make the unauthorized withdrawal if you can't." His partner was still checking his clothing to see if maybe one of the bullets had grazed him.

His partner said, "Go for it. I'm out."

James completed the last two stops and drove quickly back to the drop-off. His partner got out, slammed the door and said, "I am moving to the 2nd *Quarter*. See you, James. Be careful. Something is happening out there." He started jogging toward his car.

As the roll-up door, rolled down behind him, James got out of his rental car slowly. He was looking at the damage on both sides, with no expression on his face. The counterman was looking at James and waiting for some type of explanation. But James wasn't talking. "JAMES, what happened?"

"He left – he quit – we didn't get one of the stops withdrawals…."

The counterman spoke louder, not fully hearing James's mumblings "What?"

James still ignoring him, "Look at my rental car."

After a few minutes of calming James down, he got the full story. "Damn, do you know how much paperwork that I am going to have to do to cover your stupid 5 stops? Here, let me initial your last two stops." The counterman began printing forms from his computer and decided to wait before reporting this to his boss.

"The warnings from down South were not bogus. They told us that this was happening on the App last month. I assumed that it would stay south of us." The counterman started scrolling through FCI's Phone App. There it was a number to call if this happened.

James had been careful to buy insurance on each of his FCI rental cars but could not remember any of the details. Janet took care of most of the details. He decided to go straight home and get Janet and take her to the rental car drop off.

9

Tom Visits Old DC

Tom took the train from New POP1 to Richmond to meet with someone who could check out the stranger in KC. His *2ⁿᵈ Quarter* contacts could find very little information on the man and unless the man was a homeless hermit, something was definitely wrong.

Old DC was one of the first communities that had been renamed. It had been renamed before the Purity Purges and the *Offensive Name Act* was instituted from the Federal Government. Now the *1ˢᵗ Quarter* Administration had assumed the Federal Government's previous roles in the Eastern States.

Washington DC (the District of Columbia) was obviously renamed due to the sins of Columbus and Washington. Richmond was chosen after many arguments. Richmond was finally chosen because of its original meaning - *A Splendid Hill.* Those who worked and lived here felt very highly of themselves. No one saw the irony that although publicly being against all the "rich," most of the rich lived close to this seat of power – Richmond.

Tom had decided to meet his contact somewhere around the Old Lincoln Memorial. Joe Mack was a short stout middle manager at one of the Media Centers that monitored and controlled all Social and Platform Media.

All notations, statues and other signs of wars, soldiers, and weapons had been removed from the National Mall and the surrounding area in the midnight raids of the Morality Warriors. An unknown domestic terror attack had partially destroyed the Washington Monument years ago.

Tom Visits Old DC

The broken structure had been left by Denny Flanders. When he was elected, he stopped the privately funded restoration work.

Tom moved across the dried grass and looked up toward the large structure, and the many steps, broken in places. Only a large concrete chair – looking like a King's Throne was left in the middle of the structure.

Someone had decided that Lincoln had not had pure motives and he was removed from all history lessons and all monuments. Tents were pitched around the bottom of the concrete throne. A few small fires burned as people prepared their breakfasts.

The old National Mall area had become a large homeless encampment, so Tom had to be careful and stay on the perimeter. The *1st Quarter* had turned off all the water features including the Reflecting Pool to try to quietly discourage the encampments. Then when several National Park employees were assaulted as they serviced the few public restrooms and trash cans, the administration stopped all Park Services in the area.

Tom saw Joe Mack just off what used to be called Independence Ave. – now called Denny's Drive by the locals, in a sour satirical way. They steered clear of the restroom buildings and walked East as they talked. "Any of your guys know who this guy is?" Tom showed Joe Mack a crumpled picture of Eric Swan.

Tom had scanned and sent an encrypted picture of the stranger in KC to Joe Mack and several other contacts in the *1st Quarter*. Joe working and living in Richmond had the most access to non-public information. The *1st Quarter* could label any information non-public under their new *Free Speech Privacy Guidelines*.

Joe Mack quietly responded. "No one knows the name, but everyone knows the face. That pic you sent me, from wherever you were - is the picture of a guy that comes and goes in all the Media Centers. He has some type of security badge that allows him entrance into everywhere I go and probably more places than I am allowed into."

Tom made a face, "Oh Sh…. I wonder how many Liberty Groups have been infiltrated.

"Thanks, Joe. Do you have any other information on Financial Institutions moving out of the *1st Quarter* or just closing their doors?"

Joe looked around at the homeless shuffling by and lowered his voice. "All information is now filtered before it gets to us in the Media Centers. There are very few leaks of real information about the condition of the *1st Quarter* financials."

The two men had now walked to where they could look past the broken Washington Monument to where the White House use to be viewed. Instead of the beautiful view, they both remembered, they now could only see the 25-foot high solid wall that had been erected the length of the South Lawn.

Joe looked toward the White House and said, "I guess Denny, Gordon, and Raul got tired of looking at the mess they have created."

Tom turned to walk to his car as both men heard several shots ring out and heard sirens several blocks away.

Joe Mack walked the other direction.

10

Flanders Controls the Narrative

The administration of the *1st Quarter* had found that the easiest way to educate the citizens in the New Morality was to control all public meetings.

The Believers had been dependent upon having large meetings and singing a lot. Believers' meetings of prayer and singing did not concern the *1st Quarter* Administration. But once the Book's practices of honoring private ownership of property and independent accountability were being taught in the Believers meetings the Administration issued *The 3 Lawful Decrees*.

The 3 Lawful Decrees

The first *Lawful Decree* made it illegal for groups of more than 12 to meet for any reason without a special permit from the newly formed Climate Concern Bureau of the *1st Quarter*.

The reason the first decree was issued was because of Public Safety and Climate Concerns. No one knew who was making the rules but once the rules were "decreed" they were fully enforced by local authorities and Morality Warriors.

The second *Lawful Decree* was to control all "A" type assembly buildings. These buildings – mostly church buildings had already been approved by local Building and Safety Departments. But now due to Climate Concerns almost all independently owned assembly buildings were disallowed. If a building did get a permit to meet, they were required to report all meetings to the Climate Concern Bureau.

The third *Lawful Decree* was to resend all public meeting permits from all Believers' buildings, no matter where or when they were meeting. This was also done by the Climate Concern Bureau for the good of the climate.

The Zoning Departments of all counties were given the "scientific studies" showing that large meetings required more energy in each of the 3 areas of Climate Concern – Electrical Use, Transportation Use, and Misc. Energy Use (which included natural gas, solar and other experimental forms.)

The *1st Quarter* Media Centers were given instructions to "educate" the citizens on the importance of the 3 *Lawful Decrees* that required monitoring of all meetings in the *1st Quarter*. Social, FB (frame bot), Print and Broadcast began running similar news articles about the scientists' deep concerns about the climate and how it was being affected by these large meetings.

1st Quarter Standard Public Education

The administration had found that it was easier to educate most people if they did not know that they were being educated. Media Centers followed these guidelines.

The method:

1. Start with a deeply sincere scientist concerned about one thing or another.

> It was easy to find scientists who would say anything needed to help further their research – research which was 100% funded by the *1st Quarter* Administration.

2. Broadcast talking heads would lead with stories about the new threat and begin to copy one another. Each Broadcast Media Group tried to find their own Scientists. These media scientists could neither confirm nor deny that the threat was real. But they all scientifically confirmed that more research needed to be done.

> The Media Centers had found that they no longer needed to send news stories to each News Outlet. Most Broadcast and Print reporters copied one another's stories. It only took 4 Serious Headlines to cover the whole 1st Quarter, with hundreds of "news" stories.

3. Media Centers cubicle dwellers would use Social Media to attack, bully and post negative news about those denying the new threat uncovered by the original scientist and confirmed by the media scientists.

> Most Media Center posts were negative comments, name-calling, and threats. Generic and fictitious posts were disguised as posts of real concerned citizens.

In the past, computers had been programmed to handle Social Media bullying, but it was found that the cubicle dwellers could do a much better job posting negative comments and negative posts. The high unemployment rate ensured a large number of applicants and the job was listed as "no experience necessary."

The Media jobs were viewed as a promising career path, in an economy that required knowing someone before you could get a high paying job.

Educating the public had become an art form. Those who were the most creative with their posts and news stories were promoted to higher positions in Media Center management.

The general public no longer knew what the truth was but knew not to say anything against the newest threat. It was very dangerous to be an open skeptic with the Morality Warriors enforcing New Morality orthodoxy. Many people didn't care whether they were being deceived anymore. As long as they were taken care of.

1st Quarter Unemployment Masked

The Middle *Quarters'* unemployment was due to automation eliminating middle-class jobs that humans used to do. But the *1st Quarter* stopped all new technology 4 years ago when businesses started moving out of the East Coast central controlled economy.

The *1st Quarter* had instituted the *Job Replacement Act*. Under this act, it was unlawful to begin using new technology. The *Job Replacement Act* required all businesses to provide a Job Offset penalty or a new job to all workers who lost their jobs due to new automation. Only then would a license be given to the business so they could start using the new technology.

Of course, the Media Centers had little push back from the general public, since "social scientists" showed that every person who lost their job to automation experienced pain and a loss of income.

The Media Centers and Broadcast Centers were exempt from the *Job Replacement Act*, as was the agencies enforcing the *1st Quarter* Administration's rules and regulations.

The Media Centers were packed with employees learning to be *Cubical Dwellers* and hoping for a bright new future. The Media Centers used both computer programs and humans to post and submit "citizen" news pieces.

But a lawyer named Randy R Parris had come up with the saying, "Given only a few facts, no one can come up with a good story like a human." He rose quickly through the ranks of managers to the Top Management positions for his quick wit and total lack of ethics.

11

The Believers Go Underground

Janet and James parked and started to walk into the Equity Suites' entrance. Tom met them and nodded to the side of the building, without greeting them. They immediately knew something was wrong and went into *Option B* protocols.

Tom met them at the side of the building, "I may have been compromised in the *3ʳᵈ Quarter*. Yoga class is canceled permanently. OP-B will be handled by Jim Brooks or Hannah. I have suggested a knitting class. They will get back to us, with the where and when of the next meeting."

Janet quickly told Tom about the FCI Collector being attacked as he tried to make an unauthorized withdrawal.

Tom thought about what had happened, with the white-masked shooter. "I think it is probably random, but just in case, rent your next rental car from a new provider and stay with them. Obscure the license and I will send you a device that will block the rental car's identification system."

Janet looked to Tom, "Can you pray with James and me? He is having a real problem with this."

Tom, Janet and James, quietly and without closing their eyes prayed together and James began to relax. A sense of peace came upon all three and their minds were calmed.

After a couple of minutes of prayer, Tom said, "I have to go the Western border of the *1ˢᵗ Quarter* – maybe Old Pittsburg. I will be back in a few days and we will meet together with the group. Until then, James - don't be the trigger man at FCI – it's too dangerous.

"I will see you when the new group meets next week."

As Tom walked back to his car, one of the Believers group came running up to him. "David, what's wrong?"

David looked very worried, "Ana just called me, and they have taken Ashley."

Tom jumped into his car and yelled, "Get in. We can drive while we talk." David jumped into the passenger seat.

David continued, "Ana just called, and Children Services questioned her and somehow they are not giving Ashley back to my wife. It is at the elementary school." David was hyped up on adrenalin. "We should have never put her in that school. We were just trying to blend in."

Tom was pulling up to the school that was only a few minutes away from the Equity Suites. "This is what you do. Take this gun." Tom reached into the console between them and then pulled up and forward on what looked like a USB charging jack. A hidden compartment appeared with a gun inside.

"Go in there, get Ana and Ashely and come out the Pine Street back entrance. I will be there. Go NOW."

David Micah was a thirty-something tall muscular man that had been working as an independent contractor on scanners for DRAG Systems. His list of disillusioned business owners in the *1st Quarter* was the main database for a new underground business association.

Ana holding their baby ran out of the Pine Street entrance first, then David holding Ashley and pointing the gun back at the building. Tom had slipped one of James's old FCI masks on and was not worried about immediate detection since he was driving a fake registered older car.

These older models were being sold on the black market in the *1st Quarter* so that the Climate Tax could be avoided. The tax was 85% of the value of the car, so buying the fake registration was easier for everyone. Tom used these cars because they were invisible to the roadside scanners. Someone in the Administration was getting rich, changing the programming of the Local Law Enforcement's roadside scanners.

Tom sped away from the school and made several quick turns. Then pulled into a 5-story parking garage and drove to the 4th floor. There they changed vehicles to an older dented and unwashed station wagon.

Tom looked at David, as he got his gun back and put it into a different hidden compartment. "Get in the back - there is a false bottom. Climb in there with Ashley. There is plenty of room."

Tom started the car and had Ana put on a long black wig. Ana's hair color was blond. Then Tom said to Ana, "Put some darker makeup on those eyebrows and try to keep the baby out of sight."

As Tom pulled out of the garage, he turned back toward the school. Several dark SUVs raced past him in the other direction. "There go the Morality Warriors. Don't worry this car is fake registered and invisible to the roadside scanners."

Ana started to explain what had happened. "According to the Morality Attendant at Ashely's school, Ashely had been questioned by her teacher about the *2 Commands of Love,* of the New Morality..."

Tom shook his head, "With DRAG Systems contracting David's company, they were bound to pay a teacher to question your daughter...."

Ana interrupted, as Tom took two quick turns after driving by the school in the opposite direction. "No, it is a new mandate from the *1st Quarter* Administration. All children will be given New Morality tests twice a year.

There were 15 or 20 other children and their parents in the room that David rescued us from. They were detaining everyone to make sure that there were no Believers' children enrolled. What are we going to do now?"

Tom called Hannah on his cell phone, "Go to Micah's house and get their luggage and meet me at Fir Estates." He looked back at Ana, "Are your go-bags ready? Hannah has five minutes. Do you want her to get anything else?"

"If she could get Ashley's pink dress and the extra diapers in the baby's room, I would be very, very grateful," Ana said loudly.

"Did you hear that, Hannah?" Tom hung up quickly.

Tom was on the Interstate Highway now and took a deep breath. He drove the speed limit until they reached the exit. Tom raised his voice, "David we will be there in a few minutes. Ana throw your phone out the window."

As Tom got off the highway, he stopped and took David's phone's battery out and put the battery and the phone into a water-tight box. He jumped out and put the box behind a traffic sign just off the exit ramp.

Fir Estates was a middle-class housing track of 60 homes with 10 houses half-built in the back section. Most residents knew that the builder was not coming back to finish the houses since the new Climate Tax was levied on each new construction project. The builders who could not bribe an official at the Climate Concern Bureau had simply disappeared.

Tom drove the station wagon into the garage and jumped out and hit the down button of the automatic garage door control. Next to him, in the two-car garage was another station wagon that was also unwashed and dented.

The Believers Go Underground

Hannah pulled up a few minutes later and raised the garage door with her automatic opener. She lived here, part of the time. Tom grabbed two bags and Hannah grabbed the other two bags and they lowered the garage door again.

Hannah kept the blinds drawn all the time, except in the living room where her lights came off and on by a timer. This living room had only sheer curtains and anyone observing from the street would assume a family lived in this house.

"David and Ana, you won't be going back to your house. I assume you had your go-bags ready. Here is what Hannah got from your garage." Tom knew that all the Believers in his group lived with few possessions and they were all looking forward to the day when their mission would be over, and they could live normal lives.

David nodded and hugged his wife, baby, and daughter.

"You can stay here until we figure out what is happening. Obviously, you will be reported to DRAG Systems, so you won't be able to go back to work. Do you have the list of disgruntled business owners?" Tom took the small bound notebook from David Micah.

David said, "That's all I am carrying. I will make a full list of names of businesses who want to join the underground association of other like-minded people. I have guaranteed everyone their anonymity." David had been working hard on establishing a Business Association that was pushing for Free Markets in the *1st Quarter*.

Tom smiled, "Settle in here. It is better to home school, anyway. Even first grade has become dangerous for Believers in government schools. I will ask the group to donate some things to you." Tom stared at David and Ana and then continued, "Thank you for risking your freedom for those who want to be free."

12

Tom Warns the Liberty Groups

Tom drove West toward Old Pittsburg. He had asked Carlos from the Believers Group to come with him and bring a weapon. The four-lane highway from New POP1 was the most dangerous drive in the North *1ˢᵗ Quarter*.

Many parts of the highway only had one lane open in each direction. There were large homeless encampments along the shoulder of the highway and occasionally a child would dart into the heavy traffic. There had been more road fatalities in the last year than ever recorded as many pedestrians walked and lived on the interstate highway median strips.

Old Pittsburg was the border town to the *2ⁿᵈ Quarter* and Tom had to get the information about Erick Swan's infiltration to the Liberty Groups before they were targeted by cross-border Morality Warriors.

As they drove into Old Pittsburg, they noticed how many lines of pedestrians were slowly walking West. New cars were no longer sold in the *1ˢᵗ Quarter* and repairing older models had a high tax, due to Climate Concerns. Tom was driving a new Mercedes.

Carlos looked at Tom and commented, "It's weird right? Seeing the cars driving by as most people walk? The contrast is striking. Carlos was a thoughtful and observant and he respected Tom's balanced and pragmatic approach to the chaos around them.

Tom looked over at Carlos, "Central Controlled economies can ONLY produce striking contrasts – well said, Carlos. When a government tries to make everyone equal, everyone becomes equally disadvantaged. But of course, the ruling class must have their special treatment or who would make decisions for everyone else? They really do think they are smarter than us."

Carlos looked sadder than before, as he processed what Tom had just said. Carlos thought, "If it is true that a large majority of the *1st Quarter's* citizens have little opportunity to progress from poverty to the middle-class to wealthy - that is just sad. And without the Free Market principles of the Book being taught to the young, who will even remember the *Days of Hope*."

Carlos asked Tom, "Did you see that there are underground copies of *Days of Hope* circulating in the *1st Quarter*? I got one, but didn't leave it in my house, just in case."

Days of Hope was a new history book looking back at the Nation's previous three centuries. But it had been banned as Fake History by the *1st Quarter* and the *4th Quarter*. Rumors were that someone in Old Iowa was churning out millions of copies and flooding the West and East Coasts. Whole communities started their days finding copies laying on the many benches provided for the supermarket lines that formed each day.

Tom didn't say anything, but he knew that the Ex-Californian had a two-pronged attack with his publishing company *Freedom Books*. In just a few months there would be another free book left overnight on the supermarket benches – The Book.

Tom thought out loud, "No one is betting that people will wake up and decide to be free again. It is as hard to break an addiction to free stuff. It is as hard as breaking an addiction to drugs."

Tom pulled his car into an alley that had an open gate to the right. He carefully pulled through the narrow gate. His Charter Bank company car was a new Mercedes that would soon disappear into the *2nd Quarter*. Charter Bank would soon be taken over by the *1st Quarter* Bank Comptrollers since the plan to move out of the *1st Quarter* was in full effect.

Tom had forgotten the official name of the Act that confiscated all assets from any corporation that moved out of the *1st Quarter*. All assets officially owned by Charter Bank would be held for review to determine if the corporation had violated any banking regulations. And of course, a violation would be found by the Bank Comptrollers.

Tom jumped out of the car and walked quickly to the back door of the house. Inside he would send a warning to all his contacts in Southern Liberty Groups.

"This man (Picture attached) is an agent of the *1st Quarter* Administration and might be working for DRAG Systems."

Tom would then recommend to temporarily disappear if the group had been compromised by the man with no name - Erick Swan. Tom and everyone at Charter Bank or the Central Believers Groups would also stop and re-screen all meetings with their Liberty Group contacts.

The Believers would continue to recommend their preferences to the Liberty Groups for all political offices in the Middle *Quarters*. The plan remains the same, but all groups should relocate and increase security – they should expect cross-border Morality Warriors to attack any facility that Eric Swan knew existed.

Carlos and Tom found a rental car company that still had locations in the *1st Quarter*. Tom left his Charter Bank Mercedes in the back yard of his friend in Old Pittsburg, for the resistance's future use in the *2nd Quarter*.

They had four days to get to a safe location for the Spring elections of the *1st Quarter* in all POP centers. As they drove toward New POP3, they left the main highway. They watched hundreds of people manually pulling wagons west. Some were on riding lawn mowers, tractors or any other powered transport. Many of these had already been abandoned after running out of gas. There was no one in the eastbound lanes.

Carlos looked at the migration and back at Tom. "I wonder why the *1ˢᵗ Quarter* has not started stopping some of this migration by at least controlling the obvious places like Old Pittsburg?"

Tom smiled, "After all the talk about tearing down the Southern Wall, they would really look stupid, no matter how they would try to spin it politically."

Carlos said, "I think it is more than that. I think that the *1ˢᵗ Quarter* no longer has the money to control their Western border and they want anyone that wants to leave to leave. Some of these people have family they left in the *1ˢᵗ Quarter* and I bet they will try to help them by sending money back, once they get a middle-class job."

Tom nodded in agreement. "We just have to be careful, because there is a tipping point that happens to every unjust and central controlled economy. The citizens love to be taken care of until the government runs out of resources. Then all hell breaks loose and no one knows what to do."

They drove faster, watching for any children that may dart out in front of the rental car from the roadside camps.

What Tom and Carlos did not know was the three Top Administrators and their staffs had also concluded that controlling the Western Border of the *1ˢᵗ Quarter* would interfere with the final two Federal Agreements that all four *Quarters* were asking the old Federal Government to continue.

The old Federal Constitution had been rendered null by continued new interpretations that added or subtracted from its content or intent. When the Constitution was nullified, the first department to be disbanded was the Supreme Court – the group that had been the most responsible for destroying it.

But there were two continuing Federal Agreements that provided stability to the country. Federal Currency continuity and Federal Military Protections from foreign military encroachment on all lands of all four *Quarters*.

It was important to keep these two agreements. The *1st Quarter* Administration had concluded removing freedom of movement between the *Quarters* may bring a stop to the final Federal Agreements and chaos to the money supply.

Tom and Carlos safely returned to New POP1. But both were now worried about how long they could continue living in the *1st Quarter*. And what their escape route may look like if millions of people decided to leave the Northeast at the same time.

13

The Spring Elections

The administration of the *1ˢᵗ Quarter* normally held elections early in the year. But this year due to civil unrest the elections had been postponed to sometime in the late Spring. The announcement had been made yesterday that in 4 days the 3-year mid-term election would be held in all POP centers of the *1ˢᵗ Quarter*.

This election would be a General Election. The Primary Elections last year determined the two candidates that would be running for the Administration's elected positions. The top two candidates in last year's Primaries were the two people on this ballet. UBAP candidates had won the top two positions, so there were only UBAP candidates on the ballet.

The protests that stopped the January 31ˢᵗ General Election were started because people still remembered when they had more than one party on the ballot. This lack of choice had sparked several riots and violent confrontations with Election Officials.

Denny Flanders had run in the Primary unopposed and his name was at the top of the ballet with no other choice. Gordon and Raul were not running in this election.

Although the election date had only been announced 5 days before the election, many groups had been alerted to be ready to help "keep the elections free" 30 days ago. The Morality Warriors, Media Centers, New Morality Teachers, and other activist groups were ready as soon as the date was announced.

With the announcement of the date, the polling places were also announced. This year the official polling places were:

Any New Morality Training Building
Any Financial Counseling Center - administrating the *Right to Pay* program.
Any UBAP (United Battle Against Poverty) Registration Center

UBAP volunteers had been told which polling places they were to back-up. Since most supermarkets already had long lines just to enter the buildings, UPAB Registration Centers were moved to tables outside the supermarkets.

There was one problem. Since most FCI ARM1 locations had decided to only function on the street, UBAP volunteers did not know where to go to help the FCI polling places.

FCI Street Recruiters would go into the crowds of transients, vagrants, and pedestrians on the street and ask if anyone needed money to pay their bills under the *Right to Pay Initiative*. FCI had doubled its enrollment since using street recruitment. They had less overhead and more profit. Denny, Raul, and Gordon loved seeing more people "helped" and the numbers growing each month.

UBAP volunteers assigned to the FCI counseling centers decided to tag along with the Street Recruiters and get people to vote after the *Right to Pay* request to give out more free money.

Undercover Believers were decentralized and uncoordinated in their opposition to this sham election. UBAP officials had always felt that the end justified the means in all elections. Lies, intimidation, and deceptions were not a bad thing if it accomplished the most good for the cause. Their cause was always defined as good, so deception was always an option to help those who could not help themselves.

As more and more middle-class voters lost their jobs to businesses relocating to the *2nd Quarter*, they no longer cared about voting for more of the same. The Administration's slogan this election was MORE CHANGE. Most of the middle-class didn't think they could take much MORE CHANGE.

There was only one other active political group in the *1st Quarter* – Richards Group. This election had more tension than the last election because of the anticipation of what Richards Group might do. There were many rumors that a three-group coalition had been formed between the underground Believers, Richards Group and Liberty's Children, a group from OLD Florida.

One rumor was actually started by a *1st Quarter* Media Center "news story" based loosely on another rumor that Richard's Group had hired people to physically assault voters. The story was.

> A small group of individuals has been uncovered by Local Law Enforcement as they planned to assault people planning to vote in our free election. This group led by a shady character named Richards has planned this because he is against the free expression of political discourse. Law Enforcement assures us at Media Center 1 that they have the situation well in hand and that any attempt to hinder our free elections will be stopped.
>
> RR Paris – Media 1

The Broadcast and Cable News outlets then started interviewing "experts" on free elections and the Public Relations Officers of Law Enforcement throughout the *1st Quarter*. No one was sure of the legitimacy of the story, but everyone had a strong opinion about Richards and his band of lawless followers.

Media Center Cubicle Dwellers then picked up on the story and started posting more and more absurd comments and stories. One suggested that everyone should carry knives when they voted to protect themselves. Another posted that a large arsenal of weapons had been distributed to the Morality Warriors to defend the citizen's right to vote.

The Broadcast main news sources then reported that the Media Centers Posts were fringe group's opinions, and no one could verify the truth of what the internet was reporting. But voters should be aware that there were forces at work to stop this election and that it was, "Very, very important that everyone voted."

Anyone with an Administration job or a job that was linked to any Administration program knew they had to vote. UBAP kept names of who voted and reported back to their bosses.

Failure to vote was considered neglecting a citizen's civic responsibility. Administration managers could use the fact that you did not vote as a reason to discipline you if they did not like you.

Bi-annual employee job reviews included an employee's voting record as a reason for disciplinary action. Protections against employer abuse of employees had been established for every known behavior. But NOT voting was a reason a person could be terminated. It was becoming more and more common that, if your employer didn't like your work, they accused you of not voting.

Under the *Worker's Rights Initiative* employers could not terminate an employee for normal misconduct. The following rules had been established to protect employees under this initiative.

1. An employee may take a leave of absence for any reason and his job was secure for up to 5 years.
2. An employee may take personal time off – with pay for 10% of his scheduled shift time.
3. An employee cannot be terminated for not showing up to work after the 10% personal time has been used.
4. Time off without pay can be used for the 50% of scheduled shifts after the 10% personal time is used.
5. Any excuse can be used to not show up for work.
6. Employers cannot force an employee to work when at work.
7. Employees may file a complaint against their employer for any reason with the Worker's Rights Courts.

The Spring Elections

Everyone was planning where and when they were going to vote. The ballet was still secret, so they could vote for Fred Flintstone if they wanted. But everyone made sure that UBAP volunteers recorded the fact they had voted.

Families now posted pictures of themselves voting at the polling places to protect their jobs. Most people in the *1st Quarter* planned to get to the polls early and go home as fast as possible. No one planned on going to work on election day.

14

Richards's Resistance

Old Charlotte – now 1POP 24 was one of the headquarters of Richards Group. Richards was the last known political candidate that had run on the Freedom Platform. He had lost badly to Denny Flanders and Denny's *Right to Pay initiative*.

Since he lost to Denny, Richards had gone underground and had been working with the Southern Liberty Groups and his friends in the *1st Quarter*. Quietly and secretly many people were looking for a way to find some fairness in life. They were also tired of being shamed when calling for fairness instead of equality.

Richards's Headquarters

A tall woman announced to the small room of individuals sitting at eight computer screens. "The trucks coming from the Citizens for Independence South - carrying the Vote NO flyers have been stopped and burnt."

Richards looked over and spoke to his assistant sitting directly to his right. "Esther, call the North Liberty Groups. Ask for their help with replacing the 5 trucks coming from the South."

Most of the flyers were coming through the Northern trucking routes since most of the *1st Quarter's* population lived North of Charlotte. Richards and his team refused to use the POP Center names.

"Damn California!" Richards said under his breath.

"The current one-party system of the *1st Quarter* is a continuation of California's primary system." California had been the first in the Nation to restrict all conservative candidates by only allowing the top two primary candidates to run in a General Election.

Richards Resistance had become known by the acronym **RR** and now Richards used the **RR** on all his publications and posts. Erick Swan's infiltration of the Southern Liberty Groups had allowed him to stop Richards's shipments. The trucks that were stopped and burned last week were carrying **RR** election materials.

Richards was asking everyone to NOT Protest this election. His Flyer Read.

RESTORE
Rights
Resist
VOTE NO

It continued with detailed instructions on how to vote NO on the *No Fly Initiative*.

It then stated that if they wanted their Freedom restored DON'T VOTE for UBAP candidates and only vote NO on The *No Fly Initiative*.

On the bottom of the Flyer was a large and distinct logo **RR** that had been designed by an unemployed graphic designer. Richards's team had been branding their Resistance Movement for the last 5 years. Cheap professional work could be found in all *1st Quarter* POP cities.

Denny Flanders had decided that including his pet project of stopping all air travel in the *1st Quarter* flight paths, due to Climate Concerns was a great idea. He would immediately institute his *No Fly Initiative* no matter what the voters decided.

Denny had the right to do this because of Climate Concerns, whether anyone liked it or not. Climate "Change" and other labels had been abandoned since it was scientifically proved that no one knew what the climate was going to do in the next century.

Denny was hoping that the *4th Quarter* would follow suit as they tried to out-do him on Climate Concern issues. The *4th Quarter* prided itself on being ahead of everyone else in the country, especially on Climate Concerns. But since there were no Federal funds to rescue Southern California after *The Big One*, the once rich area was no longer a place anyone chose to live.

Richards hoped to send a message to Denny. If the majority of the populace voted NO on his *No Fly Initiative* and did NOT vote for any of the UBAP candidates, maybe Denny would begin to reconsider his agenda.

Richards was hoping that this election was the first step to restoring the rights that were guaranteed under the old Federal Bill of Rights. But Richards knew that Denny was a true believer of his own righteousness. Denny would probably try to bury the results of the election – for the good of the *1st Quarter* – of course.

Most of the flyers were printed and shipped to the POP Centers, including the three main New POP Centers last week, in anticipation of the announcement of the date of the election. The date had been given to Richards by a high-level official before the public announcement.

Now drones and 3 a.m. volunteers were ready to start a massive two-day distribution. Distribution details were sent to many Believer Groups and Liberty Groups. Some were on the Western border of the *1st Quarter* and others were undercover inside the *1st Quarter*.

In the event the cell systems and internet would be shut down on or before election day, everyone had instructions on what to do to distribute the flyers.

"Are we ready with our post-election plans?" Richards looked to Grace, the tall women moving back and forth from monitor to monitor.

"The video is edited and formatted." Grace smiled. "The street video reporters and crews in the north are ready too."

RR videographers were prepared to do their own exit polling of voters. Each interviewee would be given a white veil to cover their faces as they talked about their NO vote on the *No Fly Initiative* and NOT voting for UBAP candidates.

Richards's volunteers and undercover operatives were decentralized. Those in this room in Charlotte only knew the main distribution points. All local and regional instructions and plans were coordinated with a few men who had connections with the underground Believers groups.

Because being a believer in the *1st Quarter* meant the immediate loss of job and housing, Believers were the only fully vetted group. They could be trusted not because they felt lying and cheating were a sin. They could be trusted because they were fully underground and decentralized just to survive the Morality Warriors purges.

Now Richards was ready to confront the power structures of the *1st Quarter.*

15

Election Day

James was given the day off, due to FCI's counselors working at the polling places. Since few businesses other than supermarkets would be open, James would not have been able to collect any unauthorized withdrawals.

He and Janet had been planning to go shopping, vote, and post to social media, as all good citizens had been trained to do. Then they would go home quickly and stay home with the doors locked for the whole day and maybe the next day too.

James had picked up a **RR** paper flyer yesterday and brought it home to Janet. She then called everyone in the group with its contents. Janet explained to James that he was NOT to write Mickey Mouse on his ballet this year. They had voted for Mickey Mouse for the last three elections in protest. He was to write NO.

Janet felt it was better to go early, just in case the Morality Warriors decided the flyers had compromised the election's results and started shutting down polling places. The Administration had decentralized the polling places on this election due to the rioting of the last election. This decentralization should work to the benefit of Richards and his **RR** Flyers.

As James and Janet drove to their polling place, it was obvious that something unusual was going on. There were paper flyers on the sidewalks and pedestrians were picking them up reading them and then either dropping them quickly or putting them in their pockets.

As they stood in a line with a group of 40 people, at a supermarket 10 miles from their condo, they noticed that no one had a flyer in their hands. That was probably for the better, since by now all polling volunteers may have been informed to disqualify those possessing **RR** flyers from voting.

Denny, Gordon, and Raul were delighted to get good news early in the day. This election was setting records for citizen participation. The official exit polls were also encouraging. The *No Fly Initiative* was being approved by the citizens 99 to 1.

No **RR** drone had been shot out of the sky and the public sidewalk distribution had gone without any fatalities from the 2 a.m. Morality Warrior street checks. The time of flyer distribution had been staggered and left to each POP centers specific leaders. Many Believer groups had simply distributed flyers throughout the evening as they blended into the normal pedestrian traffic.

Drones began dropping flyers at 6 a.m., one hour before the polls opened. This tight scheduling caught the Administration's election officials off guard. The Anti – **RR** flyer Social Media posts from the Media Centers did not get fully operational until 11 a.m. Instead of deterring **RR** flyer distribution, the negative posts helped Richards's distribution, by peaking more citizen's interest.

No one in the Administration wanted to tell Denny and the other two Administrators about the **RR** flyers. So top Administration officials were unaware of the vote NO flyers until 4 p.m. Media Center top staff finally decided that not telling Denny was worse than his reaction when he was told.

Rule 12

At 5 p.m. all Administration election officials were informed to guard the election results, by Rule 12. Large vehicles were commandeered from wherever they could be found, to transport the paper ballots to a safe location. Under Rule 12 the Polling Places were closed at 6 p.m. due to safety concerns.

Instituting Rule 12 immediately changed the locations of the ballot processing centers. The Administration claimed that Rule 12 and its undisclosed guarded ballet counting locations guaranteed the integrity of the election results. Richards had a different opinion about what was happening under Rule 12.

But Richards had already been given the emergency locations by the same high-level official that had given him prior knowledge of the election's date. All 50 locations now had two *RR* operatives, using false ID already in place.

Rule 12 provided for unrelated election officials to count the ballots and then dispose of the ballots. This triple check method, of 3 strangers counting the ballots together allowed the *RR* operatives to appear as legitimate election officials. The *RR* operatives were equipped with recording devices, that could not be detected by the normal "no cell phones or recording devices" protocols.

If Rule 12 had not been initiated, Richards would not have been able to infiltrate the decentralized ballet processing centers. Ironically, Denny Flanders initiating Rule 12 to guard the integrity of the election actually did guard the true vote count.

Rule 12 mandated the following procedures to be strictly followed.

1. Four designated people called Vote Counters would enter their vote counts into the Administration's secure election system.

2. Three of the Four Vote Counters would be randomly picked to sign and send their vote counts to the Administration.

3. The ballots were immediately shredded, and the Vote Counters were required to oversee and sign off on the shredding process.

100 of the 400 Vote Counters were Richards activists and were tasked to record the correct vote count.

16

The Election Results

Tom was meeting again, with Joe Mack in Richmond. It was noon the day after the election and Joe looked tired. He had been working in two separate Media Centers since yesterday at 5 p.m. Joe had received a call that Rule 12 had been implemented and immediately reported to work.

Media teams immediately began writing, reviewing and getting approval on the reason Rule 12 had gone into effect. Back up teams began writing their stories and social posts about the election before the Administration released the official numbers.

Now Joe Mack was going home, and Tom was interested in finding out what was happening in the Media Centers. That was probably more important than the voting booths.

The vote counts had been released an hour ago. The *No Fly Initiative* passed with 78% of the vote. There had been a record turn out and Denny won 88% of the vote. Other UBAP candidates split the vote. All winners were UBAP members. No one believed the official numbers, but Joe was ready to go to bed, after being up for over 24 hours.

"So, no surprises? Everything went as expected, after Rule 12?" Tom looked a Joe. "What is the official reason for implementing Rule 12?"

"Some vague nonsense about a small group of protesters in New POP1 trying to change the vote by illegal campaigning around polling places. We had no video, no clips, and no official interviews, so it was a 'make it up as you go' moment."

"Let's get together in three days and review if **RR** flyers had any impact upon the results," Tom said. "Let's meet across the river in a residential area. I'll text you."

As Joe Mack left, Tom turned on the radio in his hotel room. He flipped around to one of the *1st Quarter Trusted News Stations* – trusted because these stations had relatives and friends of the Administration in high places. They always got the scoop before any other Media outlets.

"It is official Dennis Flanders was elected with an overwhelming majority..."

Tom always found it amazing that the talking heads all used the same verbiage and terms. He thought, "If the reporters get any lazier, they will just read the official page without comment."

Tom settled into his hotel room for the night. It was a small room off the beaten path because he wasn't using Charter Bank hotel reservations anymore. Tom's phone started to receive one text after another. It was 1 o'clock in the afternoon.

RR reveals Flanders's Election Fraud.

Tom opened his laptop and immediately saw 5 emails to each of his current email addresses. They were all the same.

Click Here to Find Out the True Election Results.

Tom clicked onto the link on the email and started watching a professional-looking video. It started with Richards standing before a **RR** – Restore Rights – Resist logo. Richards began to explain the true vote count.

As Richards revealed more about his recording of the true vote count, undercover video clips of the counting rooms and the immediate shredding of ballots showed on the screen.

Another younger woman then appeared on the screen and narrated the interviews of the Official Vote Counters – many showed their faces and gave their names. Tom assumed those who showed their faces had already escaped to the 2nd *Quarter*.

Tom turned on his TV to see what the main broadcast channels were saying. The Breaking News Banner was streaming across the bottom of the *News All the Time* channel. But the host, a popular political analyst looked confused. There were three boxes in the upper right, with three other people's faces, who also looked confused. The anchor, in a larger box and at center-left in the screen looked perplexed as he read the official Media Center *Breaking News* release.

The Administration has confirmed that Richards's vote counts are the correct counts.

> *- 5 % of the vote was cast for Denny Flanders.*
> *- The No Fly Initiative was defeated by 95% of the vote.*
> *- Although the turn out for the election was larger than any in the last 12 years, all candidates received no more than 3 % of the vote.*

The panelists, in the little boxes next to the News Commentator's head all stared blankly into their perspective cameras. They asked for the numbers to be repeated. The commentator looked even more pained to repeat the numbers.

"Wait my producer is saying that our Media Center feed has now been disconnected. We will have to wait for clarification of the vote count." The numbers were still displayed across the side panel of the TV.

After a few minutes of stumbling over their words, someone behind the scenes must have realized the numbers were still being displayed and took them down. Then the panelist's faces disappeared from the screen. Finally, the screen went black and it seemed that something had happened to the station's cable transmission.

Joe Mack had made it home and into bed with his nightly eye patches and sound machine whirring away, as all hell broke loose in the two Media Centers that he oversaw. Joe slept through one of the most important events in the last decade.

The Supreme Option.

17

Richards Hacks the Media Centers

New POP1 (and POP2 & POP3) Media Centers sent one official Administration Video to all Internet, Print and Broadcast outlets the 2nd day after the election. Media Center Oversight was at full force and management meetings were being held to "find answers."

All the Richards' videos shown on Broadcast and Cable TV yesterday were now being posted and re-posted on the internet. The major platforms licensed by the Administration had, of course, taken them down. It was their duty to follow Denny's lead and believe what Denny told them to believe. "Purity" was a prominent word in all the Major Platform's mission statements. "Purity" was defined by whatever definition the Administration Officials said it meant.

The Supreme Option

Five years before the top *1st Quarter* Administration officials had been fearful that their control over the Media Center's would be compromised and used by dissidents. Denny, Raul, and Gordon were all present when the Supreme Option was discussed.

In the event of mass civil disobedience, all Media Center's feeds and transmissions were to be hardwired to one central location. This Supreme Media Center or SMC would have the capability to superimpose *Breaking News* Banners on all Broadcast channels. All incoming and outgoing transmissions would be controlled from one location. Few people knew this Supreme Option was hardwired into all Media Centers and News Platforms.

The SMC could also break into and take over radio broadcasts. The Audio messages would begin, "We interrupt this program with important news...."

Internet feeds would also be transferred to the SMC. To protect from dissidents and lower-level employees stopping the emergency services transfer, most Media Center IT and Maintenance personnel had no idea how to reverse the Supreme Option transfer.

Richards's high-level source had first told him about the Supreme Option system two years ago. He had *2nd Quarter* journalists and real reporters within the *1st Quarter* alerted to the possibility of breaking news stories yesterday. On the Western Border of the *1st Quarter*, every broadcast and internet entity sympathetic to the Liberty Groups were ready to report on the event.

What Happened Yesterday

At exactly 1 p.m. *1st Quarter* time, the Supreme Option was triggered from Richmond. Richards sat before a fireplace with bookcases on each side. Books were deliberately placed to seem as if random. The most prominent book was *Days of Hope*, the current book of the history before the four *Quarter's* takeover from the Federal Government.

Next to *Days of Hope* sat *Brave New World* and George Orwell's *1984*. Next to this was *Animal Farm, Fahrenheit 451, Lord of the Flies* and *Pride and Prejudice.* Since these books had been banned decades before, the subtle message was lost on most viewers.

Richards began to speak in a quiet yet firm voice.

"A few decades ago, every citizen of our country had Constitutional Rights. At the end of this talk, I will put up a link for you to go and download what those rights were. These original amendments to the United States Constitution defined each citizen's individual rights (not community rights) that could not be taken away by the government.

"Our original Constitution was designed to LIMIT our government, whether city, county, state or federal. The document was written to limit the government's actions against any citizen.

"These were your rights and you have lost them. They were based upon the foundational principle that these RIGHTS come from God. And that each citizen has the Right to Life, Liberty and the Pursuit of Happiness."

Richards paused as each phrase was scrolled across the screen.

"You must choose as each generation must choose, whether you desire liberty and the freedom to pursue your own happiness. If you choose to be free you must fight to be free.

"The old United States citizens used to have the freedom to discuss freedom. We no longer have the freedom to talk about freedom. At this very moment, men are trying to stop this broadcast, because what I am saying is dangerous."

The video clip switched to Richards in one corner and one scene after the other of homelessness, the destroyed Washington Monument, long lines of those migrating toward the West... The scenes continued as Richards continued.

"You have been told that you have a RIGHT to housing, a RIGHT to medical care, a RIGHT to food, a RIGHT to have money to pay your bills. And as the government gave you each "Right," they took freedom from someone else. Every Right created by the Administration has taken freedom from you."

A detailed list of the Administration's programs scrolled down the screen as Richards listed the "Rights" that the citizens had been told were theirs.

"None of these government-created, and government-given rights are legitimate rights.

"Has the present Administration done a good job providing these Rights to you?

"When questioned, if questioned do they just say that they need more money, and everything will work out?

"You will have to decide. If you want the Right to be free, you will have to rise up against the Administration."

Now the screen changed to pictures of the present politicians and the politicians who led the country to this hopeless state.

"We do not need another leader to save us!
"We do not need another government program!
"We do not need a perfect leader!

"We need to return to the fragile equilibrium of a Free Country – Where leaders are limited in their power.

"No more useless programs that DO NOT WORK.

"NO MORE EXCUSES THAT IF THEY JUST HAD MORE OF YOUR MONEY THEIR PLAN WOULD WORK.

"WE MUST CHOOSE FREEDOM,

"IF YOU LOVE YOUR FAMILY,

"IF YOU LOVE YOUR CHILDREN,

"STOP CHOOSING SECURITY AND POVERTY OVER HOPE FOR TOMORROW.

"CHOOSE LIBERTY."

The video stopped.

2nd Quarter reporters and broadcast journalists started their transmissions using repeater stations to reach the Atlantic Ocean. Some talking heads were trying to dissect the speech. The more left-leaning political analysts were already saying nothing could be done.

Into the night and across all time zones, Richards's speech and the subjects he addressed were discussed. Only the Rocky Mountains stopped the discussion, leaving the *4th Quarter* only partially covered.

3rd Quarter **Radio Free California** continued to broadcast into the *4th Quarter* throughout the next day, giving links for anyone who would choose to learn about the fight for freedom.

People throughout the nation discussed this fight for their Lost Rights.

18

Six Months Later

We over-reacted after last Spring's election. And I think everyone would agree… that we have taken proactive steps to change the way the system works in an emergency. I have taken new responsibilities… to be the only person that can activate our emergency broadcasts." Denny Flanders was being uncharacteristically candid.

Denny was standing as he spoke, in a rare display of assertive behavior. Normally Denny sat in his seat in the middle of the raised platform of the redesigned old House of Representatives Chamber. The Chamber no longer had any hint of the past. The Relief Portraits had been taken down, along with the larger than life *In God We Trust* - compliments of the Purity Purges.

Now immediately above Denny's head was the *2 Commands of Love*.

I
Loving People means promoting Sexual Freedom and Tolerance toward all Sexual Behaviors.

II
Loving People means promoting Financial Justice and Equality for all men.

The chairs had been removed from the House Chamber, except 3 large purple Administrator's chairs in front and at the highest point of the room. Denny in the middle, Gordon on the right and Raul on the left. The staff members and local representatives from the *1ˢᵗ Quarter* were divided into three groups, depending upon their assignments. These three groups stood before three microphones – center, right and left on the lower level.

Denny sat down and Gordon spoke. "Would Frank and Sylvia please tell us about the progress of the *Right to have a Job Initiative*."

As Sylvia took the lead, staffers started taking notes. There were no cameras or other recording devices allowed in the old House Chamber – now called the Chamber of General Administration. This large room had been designed to stop all electronic signals.

By the time an attendee had entered the room, security had fully searched, scanned and body imaged him. The tight security of these proceedings was important for the health of the *1ˢᵗ Quarter*. No one ever asked why.

Sylvia spoke, "We are audience testing the name of this program that will replace the *Right to Pay* program. We have tested:

> Right to Have a Job
> Right to Work
> Right to be Employed
> Right to have enough money."

"There have been no clear winners and our Media advertising consultants feel that all our choices so far are *Wonkee*, whatever that means. We are open to any suggestions. Please send us your suggestions and we will continue to test."

Frank stepped up to the mike. "The details of how we will administer the program, once announced to the public are not fully hammered out. We need input from the 3 Administrators. Once we get a response to the 10 questions, we have sent staffers, we will need 3 months to submit a final Rules Statement."

Raul loudly stated, "Let us tentatively meet in 30 days with a complete Rules Statement. Gordon, I don't care if your staffers have to work 16-hour days. This is the most important thing we will do this year."

Gordon spoke up. "I agree, I don't think the rioting will stop until we get this program up and running. With fewer people having money to buy products and services, businesses will continue to disappear."

There had been rioting and protests in the *1ˢᵗ Quarter* since the *Right to Pay* program had been suspended. Within three months of Richards's *"Call for Liberty,"* most financial institutions had closed in the *1ˢᵗ Quarter*, except the Big 3. The Big 3 had moved into heavily guarded central locations. Security was tight and all FCI unauthorized withdrawals had been stopped.

The departure of a large percentage of the financial institutions in the *1ˢᵗ Quarter* had caused all personal credit accounts to be frozen. The licensed and loyal banks had informed Denny that over 85% of their personal credit accounts were delinquent, and it was only a matter of time.

Businesses and even the *1ˢᵗ Quarter* Administration needed the capital companies to stay loyal to the Administration and its policies. A bankrupt credit company was no good to the Administration.

Large areas in New POP1's business districts were now vacant storefronts. Most multifamily residential properties were partially vacant, and squatters were increasing in all lower-income apartment buildings.

A curfew had been in effect, in all communities of 20,000 or more since the *Right to Pay* riots started. Curfews had not stopped rioting and local authorities had instructed the police to not respond to property destruction. They were also instructed to only take reports of Felony Violence from one citizen to another. Petty crime was being ignored and many Local Law Enforcement personnel were leaving the *1ˢᵗ Quarter*.

As the House Chamber meeting continued, staffers continued with public information about the state of the *1ˢᵗ Quarter*. Raul stood, "Our final concern is our progress on stamping out the new *Die Free* group that has been attacking *1ˢᵗ Quarter* Administration facilities."

Since Richard's *Call for Liberty,* a new group had been announcing their resistance. They called themselves *Die Free* and they were as radical as the Morality Warriors. The two groups had not had a face to face confrontation yet.

Raul continued, "We will continue to use the Media Centers to label this group as *Corporate Racist,* but we need to stop them."

Denny interrupted Raul, shouting, "They use drone distribution to recruit and our Media Centers cannot control the content of the Drone Drops."

Erick Swan stood quietly in the back of the Chamber off to the side, blending into the background. An anonymous administration official had tasked him through his bosses at DRAG Systems to make *Die Free* his highest priority.

Most of the last hour was a waste of his time, but now he listened to find out additional information about *Die Free.*

Raul continued, "I would like to appoint one person from each department, to coordinate our response to any activity suspected to be from *Die Free.* Is there an agreement from my fellow administrators?" Affirmative nods came from Denny and Gordon.

Erick Swan now had a One-Stop location to find out everything the *1ˢᵗ Quarter* may know about his priority task.

As the meeting continued, one staff member after another reported upon the condition of their districts. Erick Swan thought he saw Denny snoring. Now he understood why the chairs had been removed. Half the room would be asleep.

After an hour of useless statistics only confirming the deterioration of the *1st Quarter*, the meeting was about to end.

Denny stood to dismiss the staffers. "Before we go let us all read together the 6 PRINCIPLES OF BEHAVIOR."

The room in unison, most only mumbling read.

1. I will speak and act in accordance with the 2 Laws of Love.

2. I will report all my financial transactions to DRAG Systems.

3. I am not free to speak if my words offend a fellow citizen.

4. I will be sensitive to minor requests of fellow citizens and act accordingly.

5. I will use whatever means necessary to stop those around me breaking the 2 Laws of Love.

6. My Independent Freedom should never supersede Community Freedom.

19

A New Federal Government?

After Richard's *Call for Liberty* a most interesting thing began to happen throughout the Middle *Quarters*. Although the many video streams were aimed at the abuses of power of the *1st Quarter,* the middle of the country began to talk about ending the unconstitutional rule of the 2nd and 3rd *Quarters'* unelected Administrations.

Denny Flanders had issued arrest warrants for anyone who was associated with Richards. Arrest warrants were also issued for all Liberty Group leaders. Erick Swan had a long list he had accumulated – some names were inaccurate, but no one cared.

Tom's warnings had stopped the Northern Liberty Groups from being infiltrated. But Erick Swan's list included the names of people who lived in the Old Carolinas and Old Florida. These areas, although geographically in the *1st Quarter* had not fully accepted the totalitarian rule of the Top Administrators.

The *Call to Liberty* had impacted the middle of the country more than the coasts. It had started discussions about reestablishing a modified Federal Government that would be limited to ONLY three areas of authority.

Discussions were underway about how to do this. There were daily discussion groups on *3rd Quarter* cable news stations. The larger cities newspaper editorial pages were 100% against what they called "going backward toward the old freedoms." The Star, the Register, the Gazette and the Tribune banded together to fight any effort to discuss a change. Other smaller print newspapers followed their lead by reprinting their editorials.

But there were small print news outlets that began to spring up all across the Middle *Quarters*. They were called DD's for Drone Drops since they were free and distributed by drones on an irregular schedule. As normal newspapers, tried to protect their advertising revenue by bowing to the Morality Warriors bullying, their readers rebelled. The DD's grew more prevalent.

It was these new print news outlets that could not be controlled by social bots to confuse the discussion. As people stopped listening to the hysterical angry talking heads on cable news stations, they looked forward to the next DD issue. The content was fresh and different from the controlled opinions of normal news.

The discussions were open, honest and free from retaliation. But anyone concerned with the health of the country had reoccurring problems with a strong Federal Government.

> If the Federal Government was given more power, how does that help maintain liberty?

> If there is anarchy, does not anarchy also create an undefined tyranny of the strongest?

> How much power should the Federal Government be given?

Richards was now in the middle of the country and no longer had freedom of movement in the *1st Quarter*. The Eastern border of the *2nd Quarter* was not well defined, and *1st Quarter* Administration bounty hunters roamed through the border areas looking for the Most Wanted Man.

Federal discussions in the middle of the country increased in intensity as fears of the financial collapse of the *1st Quarter* grew and what that would mean for the Federally maintained stable money supply of the whole country.

A New Federal Government?

The desire for a government that would limit government controls and guarantees the individual freedoms of every citizen had spread to every community in the Middle Quarters.

How and Why the *Quarters* Were Created

Anyone who had lived through the last 30 years had experienced some form of Federal interference in their daily lives. Most had experienced forced compliance from an unelected faceless person not from their local community.

As the Federal Government lost its legitimacy to rule, fewer people voluntarily submitted to its ever-increasing mandates and rules. The forming of the four *Quarters* Administrations was the States response to a far-off government that was viewed as representing no one.

How did this Federal decline happen? It happened over decades and its death was finalized when three separate groups decided to form a coalition to save the old United States. The first was power-hungry men and women, glad to say or do anything to obtain more power. This group joined with idealistic fools who felt their agenda was more important than the citizen's desires.

Finally, these two groups were joined by cowardly compromisers that decided it was better to get something done than do nothing. Even when the laws were detrimental to the country, they bragged about their compromises.

These three groups, the power-hungry, the idealistic totalitarian fools and the cowardly compromisers had created a Federal Government that no longer ruled with the support of its citizens. No one thought that the big Federal Government would lose its power. But it did.

Now Richards and all thinking men were confronted with this mess. Everyone agreed that answers to this mess were needed. Richard's also felt that although the answers may be initiated by a small group of men, they had to be accepted by a large majority of the people.

No one knew what the percentage of the Nation wanted a New Federal Government. But without a very large majority of the citizens agreeing on a fresh and just path, any effort to reunite the States would fail. It would require wisdom to find a path that would birth a New United States.

20

Coalitions Form To Fight Back

James had lost his job when the *Right to Pay Initiative* was closed and FCI went bankrupt. Tom asked James to accompany him on a trip to the Middle *Quarters*, leaving Janet to lead the group with Jim Brooks and Hannah.

In the event the Believers group was discovered, the final option was to be followed by each member. Janet was asked to individually give each member the final options instructions. Each member's instructions were different and would help everyone escape and hopefully survive. The Administration's control was intensifying against anyone that appeared to be disloyal to the Top Administrators.

Tom and James drove West, out of New POP1 on back roads. They were armed with James's FCI weapon and one Tom used when he was traveling. The back roads were easier to travel since there were fewer pedestrians. But they could be more dangerous. Large sections of the *1st Quarter* had no local police presence.

The areas now between the major POP Centers were lawless areas where the strongest ruled. Tom and James drove South then West to avoid the worst of the unpoliced areas. The 400-mile trip took them two days instead of the 7 hours that it would take on an unobstructed Interstate Highway.

They arrived at the Western border of the *1st Quarter* in the old Pittsburgh area with only one close call. A roadblock was perfectly hidden from Westbound traffic. Tom and James slowed with their guns hidden in their laps.

The sun was setting behind the guard - a 15-year-old boy. As the boy looked inside and saw two handguns pointed at his torso, he stepped back. Tom quietly said, "We don't have any money. We would like to pass without a firefight."

The boy appeared to be alone and nodded. Tom maneuvered around several disabled vehicles that had been positioned in the middle of the highway to slow Westbound traffic.

Tom and James's success had not been due to luck. Tom had extensive contacts throughout the Lawless Areas and had followed a path that most people did not know existed. If the weather had become bad, they would have been delayed a week or more, since Tom's route to old Pittsburg took them off-road several times.

Once in the *2nd Quarter*, Tom headed to Columbus with a valid *2nd Quarter* ID and special *2nd Quarter* letters of intent. It was strange for James to visit Columbus since James had been taught that names must not offend anyone. The name Columbus was only whispered in the *1st Quarter*.

The highway trip from the old Pittsburg area to Columbus only took 3 hours. Tom took this opportunity to help James process the culture shock he was about to experience in the Middle *Quarters*.

"It isn't the names of things that we need to worry about. It is what is in people's hearts and how that affects their actions. That is what we have to worry about." Tom roughly paraphrased a phrase from The Book.

He continued, "The truth of history can only be maintained by keeping facts - facts. If something is true, it is true and there is no reason to hide from it."

Tom continued, "Instead of the *1st Quarter's* quote that you have been taught – ***If government is not working, give them more money.***"

Coalitions Form To Fight Back

James nodded. He knew that one.

Tom continued, "Instead of that stupid quote, here is one that makes sense." Tom roughly paraphrased a quote that most people had forgotten.

*"Those who cannot remember the past
are condemned to repeat it. "*

James had lived most of his adult life believing that history should be avoided if it offended anyone. Now Tom was confronting one lie after another and James's head was beginning to hurt.

Tom saw James's perplexed look and changed the subject to how the group in New POP1 was doing and James's relationship with Janet.

Tom and James met representatives of 4 groups in Columbus. The representatives were very interested in a gathering to discuss a New expanded Bill of Rights and maybe a new Federal Constitution. This trip was one of many trips being done by men wanting to form coalitions to see if it was possible to see any document that resembled the old Bill of Rights.

The first group was The Northeast Liberty group. It was made up of agnostic Libertarians. Their position was that we should not allow the Federal Government to regulate anything, period. Their written comment given to Tom was that a preamble should be attached to any new Bill of Rights. **"We mean it this time."**

The second group was The DD group (Drone Drops). It was made up of creative young men and women who had committed their lives to the truth. Their main enemies were government Media Centers and other media outlets that profited from reporting distorted facts.

The third group was The North Central Believers group. They were Believers in The Book. They wanted Tom to report that the original

Declaration of Independence should be stressed. Tom agreed and knew that the strength of the Declaration was why it had been banned from history books decades ago.

The last group that Tom and James met with was two men representing 11 States in the *2nd Quarter*. They had been appointed to represent the redrawing of 11 state boundaries of the *2nd Quarter* and discussed how State governments would be impacted by a newly formed Federal Constitution.

Tom met with each group and listened to each group's concerns, worries and fears. He established lines of communication with each group and was assigned a special DD landline to those in the North Central area.

Tom and James continued across the 2nd and 3rd *Quarters*, avoiding the South Liberty groups that had been sloppy and allowed Erick Swan to have access to their leadership's identities.

After one month of travel, Tom and James arrived in the middle of Iowa. They had a list of groups in the *2nd Quarter* that were interested in discussing a Revised Federal Constitution that could be ratified by the middle of the country.

21

The Bethany Assembly

The speaker looked out across the group of 500 men and women and began. "Welcome, I am Craig Carmichael and I was chosen to address you and coordinate this Assembly's thoughts, so we can have a timely and clear communication of our ideas."

"Whether you all come to conclusions about anything in the next week is up to you, not me nor those who organized this meeting. Please share your thoughts and opinions with us."

"The following responses came from you and I will put them on the side projectors and also on your terminals."

SoMo Banking had installed a closed system that provided 300 terminals that were interactive but not connected to the internet.

Craig continued, "We ask that you do not use any outside devices when discussing these meetings. There are others watching and participating as you know, and they have also been asked to keep these meetings secret."

Craig clicking a button in his hand, started his 5-minute summary. "The reasons that YOU stated we need a revised Federal Government are…" He read from the large overhead projectors.

I. We no longer have freedom of movement from community to community.
    A. A lack of safety along all border areas.
    B. Some cities now building barriers to control traffic in and out of their city.
    C. Law Enforcement no longer has clear jurisdictions.

II. The stable money supply may disappear with the Federal Government's authority further eroded by the financial failures of the 1st *Quarter*.

    A. The upper Minnesota break-off now only accepts *Riols,* their own currency.

    B. The exchange rate between the *Quarters* is no longer reliable.

    C. Without a stable money supply, our economy will become too volatile to maintain stable capital investments.

    D. A stable money supply and stable government is the one thing that a free market economy must have to be a free market.

III. Our Military may be used against our own citizens while losing its ability to protect us from foreign actors.

    A. There are rumors that Central and South American interests have been considering moving into West Texas and South Florida.

    B. The natural resources of Alaska are being mined by Asian Companies with no right to ownership.

    C. Hawaii is no longer allowing Military bases that provide security to our Western Coastline since the *Hawaiian Sovereignty Act* has instituted DNA testing of all voters and suspended all non-natives from owning or using land.

"Please enter your 3 letter Acronym on line one and then respond with an agreement to these points…."

The Bethany Assembly

Security was tight in Bethany Missouri. The approximate geographic center of the Middle of the Nation. Bethany was small enough to control all visitors. It also had a large military presence two hours away, at the KC Intermodal.

Federal Military Security had been moved into strategic field positions around Bethany. The Army Reserves based in KC were called up to coordinate the security of this Assembly.

A large church, next to the old Assembly Church had been built several years ago when a large percentage of the city had converted and became Believers. This church was now being used for the attendees. The large trustworthy population of Believers was another reason Bethany was chosen as a secure site.

Two hours north there was a mixed academic population that was always confused about all matters of government. Two hours South was a larger population that wanted the Fake Rights of the *1ˢᵗ Quarter* instituted in their communities. These two groups were strongly against the reason for these meetings.

One month ago, Bethany locals were given new city ID's. Highways in and out of town were rerouted around Bethany. The Army Corps of Engineers had created an Interstate Highway Bypass around the town, although the 25 MPH speed limit had not been appreciated by north or south travelers on I-35.

Tom had asked his trusted Middle *Quarter* contacts to be a part of the coordinating teams for this event. Charter Bank had financed all housing in local hotels. Extra housing had been moved into place two weeks ago and the City Water System had been upgraded by Community State Bank.

All groups had been asked to send *Inquiry Response Form One* if they wanted to be included in the discussions. No one had high expectations for these meetings. And most were fearful of some type of attack against their group. Many top leaders would be watching from undisclosed locations on a secure Military hardened landline that was installed many years ago to withstand a nuclear attack.

No contact information was attached to any form or questionnaire. Contact information was held by the Ex-Californian, in encrypted files. Tom's team had been tasked with interfacing with 24 groups.

He had personally met with each of his group's main contacts. Two other teams had also been assigned 24 groups making a total of 72 groups participating.

Inquiry Response Form One

1. Why do you want to support a new Federal Constitution?
2. What would be the one change that would cause you to stop supporting a new Federal Constitution?
3. What would you include in a new Bill of Rights?
4. What would you delete from the original constitution?
5. What are your other concerns, ideas, and desires?
6. What is the next step you would consider?

Everyone will have the freedom to expand, change or add to your responses as these discussions continue.

Groups were asked to answer these six questions. Four separate and isolated groups of DD editors from Drone Drop News had assembled one week earlier to sort and categorize the comments. They were promised a full report when the Bethany Assembly was concluded.

All DD publishers were vetted and invited to the meetings, with the understanding that they must not publish until the meetings were concluded. They were given terminals in the Old Assembly building next door to assure privacy to the attendees.

Craig continued, "Everyone here has initially agreed upon the Three Points of why we need to do something about our present circumstances of Government. Now we will have to discuss **What to Do**."

Another man stood next to Craig and began to speak. "Now we want to review with you - your responses about what may be our course of action going forward. What you sent as the Next Step, question 6."

You will notice the response percentages after each question. These are loosely worded summaries. Other topics may be important, but we had to address those topics you said were the most important first." He pushed a button on the podium.

NEXT STEPS
1. Define new State boundaries.   85%
2. Define specific wording of the Bill of Rights. 78%
3. Define how government can be limited.   76%
4. Define the powers of the branches.   55%
5. Modernize the original Constitution.   52%

Craig continued, "We will begin hearing from the different groups that are being represented here today."

The First Group's spokesman approached the mike.

"My name is Hunter and I am one of the Pastors of the church that meets in Bethany and Harrison County. I have been asked to address you first and share the *3rd Quarter* Believers' concerns. I know there are other Believers groups here and I do not speak for them."

A young longhaired man stood next to Hunter and began typing into a terminal next to the podium. As he typed, the large Projection Units and all terminals mirrored Hunter's points, as he spoke.

"Number one – We do not want and do not need a Supreme Leader if or when we have a legitimate Federal Government. We do not feel looking to an Administrator as some do in our divided country is the answer.

"Number two - We do not want and do not need a Believer to be elected as our Federal President. But we will fight for all leaders to observe the morality of the Book and not the New Morality.

"Number three – We HAVE to have leaders who have integrity and do not lie to us. A man's personal life is between him and God. But we need leaders who do not lie, cheat, steal or hide their agendas."

Hunter, a 40 something man with prematurely graying hair sat down. Each speaker would have initially 10 minutes to address the Room. Hunter had taken only 1 minute.

Craig stood and reached into a basket full of slips of paper. Pulled one slip out and asked for the Representative from the Citizens for Independence – South to address the Room.

An older man with a trimmed white beard and dressed casually slowly approached the podium from the back of the room. He did not smile, as his lean frame moved across the platform.

"I am… Jack... My name is not important. Hello to the Patriots in the South. Keep the Faith."

He waved to the Camera to his left.

"I represent the Citizens of Independence - Southern District. We held things together and have been fighting the forces who have turned our country into the mess it is in now.

"Brave men and women have stood together to fight the Purity Purges. We stopped all name changes in our communities. We stopped all destruction of art and other educational materials. We stopped all destruction of historical monuments.

"And we stopped the *2nd Quarter* government officials when they came to stop normal civil order and enforcement of accepted laws. They were weak. And they were too scared to fight. We used guns to fight back. Guns that the constitution that you are NOW trying to change guaranteed us we could have - so we could remain free.

"I agree with what the Pastor just said, and I agree that this is an emergency. Those in my area know that the *1ˢᵗ Quarter* is now stopping people from bringing any property with them as they try to move to our still Free Southern Lands...."

This man continued to talk about the things that the South *2ⁿᵈ Quarter* was experiencing, and the DD editors were frantically trying to keep up. There was not a lot of news from this area.

"South of Atlanta – and don't try to make me call it POP23 – There are roadblocks on all major highways trying to stop thousands of people escaping Florida.

"There are rumors of South Florida communities no longer belonging to our country and deciding to go with a Newly formed gulf government.

"We need help since Huntsville, Murfreesboro, and the western communities of Atlanta have a large population of families trying to be free from the Tyranny of Flanders and his stupid, stupid administration...."

A light started to blink next to him – since he had used up his time. But he continued, "Turn that damn thing off."

"We have stood with courage to stop the damn deterioration of our communities and we need help if we are going to succeed.

"I know you all can't put a courage clause in our elections. But it sure would be nice if we could stop electing fools and cowards...."

He finally stopped and apologized for running over his time. By the time he was done, many in the room had tears in their eyes. Although a little rough around the edges, no one doubted his sincerity and his truthful accounts of the *2ⁿᵈ Quarter* Administration's failures.

Craig slowly got up, composing himself and pulled the next slip from the basket. "Would the Sons of Liberty – Indiana representative like to address the Room?"

A clean-shaven man in his 50's stood at the platform, visibly shaken. He looked down at the man who had just spoken and said, "Thank you, we are grateful to all your group and their courage to stand against the tyranny of the majority and maintain personal freedoms."

"I am Mike, and this is my wife Camile. We represent the leaders of a large Liberty Group based in Indiana. We would like to speak together."

As Mike reached out his hand to his wife, Camile spoke, "Our concerns are whether we can balance the power we give to the Federal Government and stop this idea that it needs to fix everything."

She was an average height slender woman and she continued. "If we are to do this, if we are to go back to a limited Federal Government, we MUST build strict limits to its authority."

Mike continued as if the couple was used to talking as a tag-team. "The DD news has had many discussions and forums about these limits. It is my feeling that we should be careful to NOT abrogate our opinions to a group of experts. That is what got us into this mess."

Camile picked it up, "History is great and History Professor's opinions should be listened to. But then we should use our own life experience and common sense to avoid the stupidity of Expert Opinion Syndrome. We have been told too long that our opinions take 2nd place to the expert's opinions."

The light began flashing, but Craig quickly turned the timer off and back on. He jumped up and stated, "Since there are two, we will reset this." Everyone in the room agreed. They seemed to be mesmerized by the way Mike and Camile tag-team talked.

Mike said, "I am sorry, we will wrap this up soon. It is my group's opinion that the Bill of Rights must include strict protections from the government. We fully agree with Richards *Call for Liberty*. Our first Right should be FREEDOM FROM GOVERNMENT...."

Camile jumped in, "And we should CONFRONT every politician who tries to create a right for one person that will take a right from another person. All people should have the same rights. PERIOD."

The room broke into applause. Everyone in the room had been deeply affected by Richards *Call for Liberty*.

When the couple was done, Craig Carmichael stood and continued to direct which speaker would address the Assembly. After 2 hours had elapsed, he said, "We should take a break here. Let's come back in one hour and we will continue. Take this time to communicate with your groups and see if there are clear items you would like to add to the discussions."

As the day progressed, each spokesperson addressed issues of concern from their group. The DD reporters in the building next to the assembly continued to chronicle and summarize the Assembly's speaker's comments.

22

Raul's Ambitions

Captain Briana Pomposa was assigned to the oversight of the *3rd Quarter* Army Brigade Combat Teams – BCT. Captain Pomposa's political position was for a strong Federal Government. Her politics were similar to most of those who were still employed by the Federal Government.

Briana was now on a secure video communication with 3 men in Richmond. Roachman, one of the *3rd Quarter* politicians sat with her at the same computer terminal.

Briana talked to the screen. "We can keep you all informed about the progress in Bethany. Getting someone into the area to participate will be difficult."

The three men sitting on the opposite end of this call were opposites in personality types and communication.

Raul – one of the three *1st Quarter* Administrators spoke first. "I am sending 3 people and I want them not only transported safely but on the agenda to speak. Just get it done."

Raul's approach was rough and loud. The man sitting to his right quickly jumped in when he saw Raul was done trying to bully Briana, as he bullied all women in his employ. "Captain, Arne Nelson here. We really appreciate your help with this, and I know you will do your best to see our mission succeed."

Arne Nelson was a six-foot five-inch, lean 50ish man that had succeeded as the CEO of one of the only four Hotel Chains that survived the DRAG Systems take over the *1st Quarter*.

Raul's Ambitions

Arne grew up a marginal Believer when marginal believers existed in the Free United States. He quickly converted to the New Morality when the *1st Quarter* established the New Morality Centers.

Arne's biggest skill set was saying something that sounded very smart but had no real meaning. He could get most people to follow his lead by this ability to communicate nonsense with sincerity and conviction. He now was helping Raul and DRAG Systems try to salvage what could be a major setback – a New Bill of Rights.

Raul glanced to his right, with an annoyed look. Raul had decided he should make his play for more authority before Denny Flanders decided to get rid of him. Raul had given Richards the Security Information he had needed to disrupt the election count reporting.

Raul had shared Rule 12's Vote Counting Centers' locations, allowing Richards the opportunity to monitor the real election results. Raul had personally given Richards the Supreme Option codes transferring all Media Center transmissions to only one Media Feed.

If there was to be a New Federal Government, Raul wanted to be one of the powerful and not one of those on trial for his actions as a top Administrator of the *1st Quarter*.

Erick Swan looked at the two men sitting next to him. Each man sat at their own monitor. The physical difference was striking and a little silly. Raul, short and fat sat higher than the tall lean Arne Nelson. Raul's assistant had made sure that Raul's chair was higher than everyone else's chair before the meeting began.

Erick looked down and realized that Raul's feet were not touching the floor. Since there were only three men in the room, he realized that Raul was not just vain but also dangerously stupid.

Erick Swan spoke up, directing his comments to the man sitting next to Captain Pomposa, "Roachman, good to see you again."

Erick Swan continued talking to everyone, "We need to push for central control of all social programs. DRAG Systems cannot maintain proper oversight of the economy if new Federal Social Programs are decentralized."

Arne waited patiently, "Yes, that is a number one priority. How can anyone argue against the New Morality's Rules? How can anyone not want a culture rooted in love?" Arne's strength was to state the obvious with conviction. His second strength was to change the meaning of any word, from its original meaning and still sound intelligent.

Erick Swan continued, "All the politicians of the Middle *Quarters* who have been invited to these proceedings should be given this. Write this down. Everyone should want…"

> "1. An atmosphere that fosters diverse opinions.
> "2. Speakers who approach issues with an open attitude.
> "3. They should strive for constructive disagreement."

Arne got excited, "That is great. Where did you get that? How can anyone disagree with open discourse?"

Raul cut Arne off, still looking annoyed with him. "And after all the disagreement and diverse opinions, I want to know who is on our side and who is not. We need names and addresses."

He took a deep breath. "And everyone who does not want a strong, central controlled government should be called what they are – hate-filled, racist, immoral men who do not understand the meaning of justice or right behavior."

"We may have to listen to hateful speech from the greedy and the selfish, for these discussions, but we should take notes and shut down their evil speech as soon as we can."

Erick Swan was not done but realized he had to defer to Raul's position. Erick Swan jumped in when it looked like Raul was taking a breath. "DRAG Systems wants to make sure that any new government has Social Justice and Social Program powers. Central controlled financial programs allow them to monitor…"

Raul was angry and starting to recognize that when he helped Richards, he may have opened a *"big can of trouble,"* as they say in his Workers Rights - hometown.

"Briana, I will be sending Arne and Erick Swan to help you with your mission in Bethany. Please meet them in KC, tomorrow. I will send a Workers Party advance teammate to the designated place. Her name is Sarah Franks – Roachman you will recognize her."

Raul pushed a button before anyone could acknowledge what he just said. Jumped off his highchair and walked briskly from the room. Erick Swan and Arne blankly looked at each other.

23

The New Bill of Rights

The first day of the Bethany Assembly had ended at 11 p.m. Every politician had run over their time and many had said nothing when they were talking. The day had started with excitement and ended with prayers for silence.

Craig Carmichael took the stage at 10 in the morning, when most of the terminals were manned by at least one representative. Tom noted who was not there from his groups and sent James to find the missing representatives.

Craig started, "We will be dividing into two groups depending upon the *Quarter* you now represent. If you feel that your group would like to be included in both *Quarter's* discussions on the new State geographic boundaries, please send representatives to both meetings.

"Since we will be streaming and conferencing tomorrow's meetings on State Boundaries, we will continue to meet in this room. 8 a.m. to 2 p.m. will be - *2nd Quarter* States and 3 p.m. to 9 p.m. will be *3rd Quarter* States."

As Craig continued, the Ex-Californian and another man climbed up the steps to the platform. "Today we will be discussing a New Constitution and what that might look like. Here to review what is now on your screens is Ja'Ron Stewart from former SoCal and the writer of this rough draft."

Ja'Ron's father had not escaped the Big One and Ja'Ron had moved from Denver to Iowa when Denver changed its name to 3POP4 and imported West Coast politicians. Ja'Ron had stood with the Believers south of Denver, as Old Colorado had split in half from West to East roughly along the line of Interstate 70.

The New Bill of Rights

South Colorada continued to elect Liberty Party candidates. The northern half of the State elected West Coast candidates who immediately instituted strong controls on all business and religious teachings, loosely aligned with the New Morality.

Ja'Ron addressed the assembly, "Most of you don't know me, but I stood with the South I-70 resistance in Old Colorado and we held the line. DRAG Systems does not monitor anything South of I-70 accept a small area around 3POP4 – Old Denver."

"I am here to start this discussion on the New Constitution that you now see on your screens. It is divided into 10 sections – which you may decide to change, add or eliminate as you see fit. Please wait and electronically submit your changes later."

The overhead projectors on the right and left of the platform were turned on with the following text.

Principles of Federal Freedom

The following principles may or may not be instituted to limit the Federal Government's ability to interfere in the lives of the citizens that it is supposed to be serving.

Section 1 – The Bill of Rights
1. The Bill of Rights is the first Principle and is written to restrain the government's actions.
2. The Bill of Rights defines all "rights" guaranteed by Section 1.
3. The Bill of Rights cannot be amended without amending this whole document.
4. The Bill of Rights will detail what the government can NOT do to any citizen.
5. The Bill of Rights cannot be superseded by lower government entities. It dictates first Principles to State, County, and City.

Section 2 – Regulations and Laws

1. No regulation of US business, US citizen or US corporate entity will be passed without an 85% vote of the legislature.

2. No regulation of US business, US citizen or US corporate entity will be broad or assigned to any agency without specific requirements within the law.

3. No regulation of US business, US citizen or US corporate entity will be instituted without a four-year review of its unforeseen impact, its success or its failure.

4. 45% of the legislature may call a Review Vote at the four-year review and terminate the law with a 51% majority vote.

5. No regulation of business, citizen or corporate entity will be passed without a seven-year sunset provision with a firm date of termination of the law and all its requirements.

6. Regulations, foreign treaties, tariffs and other forms of controlling foreign investment, foreign imports or exports and foreign entry and exit can be passed with a 51% majority. No higher bar will be set to protect or control foreign and border concerns.

Section 3 – Taxes, Fees & Misc. confiscation of property

1. All laws creating taxes or fees will be passed by 76% of the legislating bodies members.

2. All laws creating taxes or fees are required to have a ten-year review of the law and its unforeseen impact.

3. 45% of the Legislature may call a Review Vote after five years and review and terminate the law with a 51% majority vote.

4. All laws creating taxes or fees must designate what the tax is to be spent for and what it is to accomplish.

5. All taxes and fees cannot be diverted to other programs without a 76% vote of the legislating body.

Section 4 – Three Mandates of Federal Government

1. Mandate - to oversee the stability of the money supply, currency and exchange rates set by financial institutions.

2. Mandate - to guard and oversee Federal borders.

3. Mandate - to oversee the Military and its operations.

Section 5 – Social Programs and Charity

1. The Federal Government will not institute, direct, create or administrate any Social Programs as defined in Section 5.

2. A Social Program is defined as any law or provision that requires the Federal government to distribute funds to any private citizen or group of citizens for any reason.

3. These Social Programs include but are not limited to the now-bankrupt Social Security Insurance, Medicare Funds, Medicaid Funds, Survivors Funds, Disaster Relief Funds, and/or National Flood Insurance Funds.

4. The Federal Government delegates all powers and rights to establish, administer and maintain Social Programs, Charity or other Funds to the State and Local Governments.

Section 6 – Elections

1. The Federal Government will not oversee elections.

2. State Governments will regulate and oversee all elections.

3. Term limits for all Federal Candidates. One Term only.

4. One man, one vote will not be used to elect specific Federal positions as outlined by Section 6.

Section 7 – States Boundaries and States Rights

Section 8 – Checks and Balances – Branches of the Federal

Section 9 – Judicial Branch Restrictions

1. Federal judges will be appointed for 10-year terms and cannot serve in any other judicial position after the term limit.

2. No Regional Federal Judges or lessor Federal Judges will be appointed.

3. State Government Judges may submit Federal cases directly to the Federal Court.

4. The Federal Court has only one job - to decide whether a law conforms to and follows the intent of the Bill of Rights and this Constitution.

5. The Federal Court may rule with an "up or down" vote - but cannot force any action other than to stop or continue the law under review.

Section 10 – 1787 Constitution and New Ratification Processes
    1. Define what wording should be kept from the 1787 Constitution not addressed by the previous Section 1 through 9.
    2. Designate and define areas that are no longer needed and why. (example: the last 10 years of no U.S. Postal Service has produced cheaper, faster and better service.)
    3. Designate the process to ratify this new Constitution.

The room erupted in many conversations and comments as the groups read the *Principles of Federal Freedom* from their screens. Ja'Ron Stuart began reviewing the different section's bullet points.

"Drafts of the new Federal Constitution will not be released until you comment on these guidelines. We ask you to submit detailed wording from your groups."

The Ex-Californian stood as Ja'Ron stepped to the side. Ja'Ron remained standing next to him.

"Some of you may feel that these restrictions upon the Federal render it helpless to help us. Since a large Federal Government that tries to solve all the problems of its citizens has been tried and failed, we must ask ourselves, 'How much do we want to be helped?' You will have to decide.

"We may not have another chance to find the order of government as chaos continues to expand throughout our Nation. It is the time to have courage, as our founding fathers had the courage and decide that the future of our children's freedom is now in our hands – literally.

"Let us intelligently discuss these principles of government. These issues need to be addressed in this series of meetings and no longer put off to a more convenient time. "NOW is the time."

24

Erick Swan Infiltrates Bethany

Roachman had met Sarah Franks in a quiet neighborhood south of the Airport in KC. Captain Briana Pomposa dressed in full uniform met Arne and Erick Swan's flight. They were traveling commercial coach together as *2nd Quarter* businessman out of the South *2nd Quarter*.

Captain Pomposa drove the two to a house that Sarah Franks had rented last year, although no one had actually lived there for more than a week at a time. It was a Workers Party coordination house.

As they entered the house, it was obvious that no one lived there. Suitcases, backpacks and duffle bags were stacked to the ceiling along one wall of the living room. The kitchen had stacks of MRE's on one wall and misc. canned goods along another wall.

As Arne began opening a door to use the bathroom, Sarah commanded, "Don't go in there!" Arne jumped back.

Sarah directed, "The bathroom is down the hall to your left. You don't need to see what is in that room."

When Arne got back from his bathroom trip, Captain Pomposa spoke first, "My job is to get you into the Bethany Assembly area – past 3 security checkpoints. It should be relatively easy, but if something happens, you are on your own. I am not providing security, only transportation."

Roachman, a *3rd Quarter* politician from the Kansas side spoke, "I think it would be better if I took Arne as a part of my staff." Roachman had left Bethany at 5 a.m. to pick up a sick staff member.

Pomposa continued, "I will escort you, Erick, 3 hours after Jim and Arne leave. I have a uniform for you to wear."

Erick asked, "Does it have a cover? My face may or may not be recognized at the checkpoints. I will use a scar and a few tricks for the facial recognition scanners, but a cover would be great too."

"Yea, our full uniform requires a hat, but don't call it a cover or security will realize you are not from around here. In fact, don't say anything." Pomposa replied.

Erick continued, "I have three bags. Arne, you only have one. Can you take two of mine and I will stuff my other stuff into a seabag, ahh – I mean duffel. Looking at Sarah, "You have an extra duffel?"

Sarah Franks nodded toward the living room wall stacked with every kind of bag, many from military units not from the 3rd *Quarter*. "Take whatever you need. Leave whatever you are not going to use."

Sarah Franks had fought in the Progressive Anarchist groups of KC for over a decade. Now she was coordinating the Morality Warriors efforts to institute the New Morality in as many cities as they could in the 3rd *Quarter*.

Erick Swan grabbed the two rolling bags that had been smuggled onto the plane in Richmond. He helped load them into the newer model BMW Jim and Arne were taking to Bethany. Erick was younger than Arne or Jim and the space to load in the closed garage was tight. It was natural that Erick Swan would help load the bags.

Erick spoke, "Arne, I will pick these up from you, once I change into civilian clothes in Bethany. Roachman can show us where we are staying."

Roachman nodded affirmatively.

Erick Swan Infiltrates Bethany

Roachman and Arne got into the BMW and before the automatic garage door lifted, Erick retreated to the house. All the neighbors saw, if any were watching was a car with two men leaving the house. Sarah Franks clicked her automatic door button and the door lowered loudly.

Erick Swan sat down to wait and didn't say a word for the next three hours. The two women talked quietly in the kitchen. Sarah was naturally curious and had a hard time not asking Erick Swan questions, disguised as small talk. But after a few awkward non-responses, she left Erick Swan alone.

At 8 p.m. Erick Swan and Captain Pomposa arrived at the motel in Bethany, without incident. He jumped out as Briana pointed at his Motel. "Remember you are…."

Erick Swan was already walking away.

Captain Briana Pomposa returned to her office and completed the day's paperwork that had piled up on her desk. She thought, "Hopefully these guys can help moderate any radical ideas of the Middle *Quarters*."

25

Clark Williamson

Everyone was in their seats early the next morning at the Bethany Assembly. Yesterday's meetings on State boundaries and State's rights had been long. But although tired, everyone was now waiting for one of the few celebrities that people still trusted in the Middle *Quarters*.

The organizers had asked Clark Williamson to speak this morning because he always drew a crowd and today was no exception. Clark had gladly accepted. He was not a part of any special Liberty Group. He was not a politician and had never been elected to anything. This gave him more credibility to most of the attendees.

Clark Williamson's nightly cable program was one of the few still being produced without government censorship. Mainly due to the Middle *Quarter's* love for the truth of his message. Most cable news programs just repeated what the Media Centers or large Print Publications reported. The more ambitious cable news programs tried to amplify whatever story was released with their own content.

Since no one believed anything that was reported in the day's news cycle, millions of people waited to hear what Clark thought about the newest controversy or Media Center crisis. Clark had friends throughout the country who fed him real facts and observations.

Each day news outlets reported one crisis or fabrication after another. Some speculated that they were just going for the highest ratings. But the more skeptical thought they were just lazy.

Each day a reporter somewhere reported that "If something was not done by the government, the world as we know it would collapse."

Like in the story of *The Boy Who Cried Wolf*, no one paid any attention any longer. Ironically the Federal Government before its full disintegration had banned the story of *The Boy Who Cried Wolf* from all textbooks and libraries. It had something about offending wolf lovers and portraying wolves in a bad light.

Now Clark Williamson was about to take the stage. There was standing room only. Clark, looking younger than his 46 years, climbed the steps to the stage quickly and glided across the platform, smiling with his trademark coy smile.

"They're morons," he started. The room erupted with quiet laughter. Clark had won the hearts of a nation of freedom-loving people, by calling morons – morons. Something that the fearful and the timid had long since avoided.

He continued, "Thank you for inviting me to this gathering. I am honored that you would consider me as a speaker at this very important event." Clark's courage to speak the truth was his greatest strength. His second strength was true humility. Instead of pretending to be honored, he really felt honored.

Clark was a believer, but most who watched his nightly program knew nothing about his personal beliefs. His arguments were thoughtful and intellectually honest.

A few minutes before, he had been sitting on the front row and had mouthed this prayer. "God help me speak truth. God help me be clear. God help me."

He continued, "I have read the 10 Sections of *Principles of Federal Freedom* and next week, once you all have left Bethany, I will produce a week of programs from this room. I will talk about these principles and have some of you on the program if you agree to appear."

Clark took a drink of water and continued. "We have all seen the chaos, the stupidity and the harm that has come to the nation by government deciding that it must address and fix every problem."

"As you proceed this week, consider asking the government to NOT fix our problems; NOT take care of us and NOT do more than it is asked.

"Consider asking our future government to RESTORE the order of law that protects the individual rights of each citizen…
Protects our safety from real – not imagined – criminal actions…
Protects our right to our own property and what we can do with it…
A government that in most cases LEAVES US ALONE."

The Assembly erupted into applause. And there were many shouts of "Amen" and other positive comments. The poorer the area that a representative represented the louder they applauded. It had been the poorest who had suffered the most, as the government tried to fix every problem with a new regulation or tax.

Clark paused to let the shouts die down and continued, "Today we have a great opportunity to disagree until we agree. We must come to an agreement. We may not like all the ideas of the person sitting next to us. But there is a possibility that they may be right, and you may be wrong. Or you may be right, and they may be wrong. Let us respect one another enough to listen and argue until we come to an agreement.

"Let us stop acting like we know everything and just say what we know and define why we believe what we believe. Being free means being free to say what we feel without the fear of being punished by those who disagree with us.

"Let us agree that none of us are here to win an argument. We are here to save a nation...

A large blast destroyed the platform area and everyone on the platform was immediately killed. The large room filled with smoke and those who could - ran for the doors, fearing another blast.

Tom was next to one of the front-side doors and found himself outside but could not remember how he got there. As he looked up, he saw the man he had seen last year in the KC intermodal meetings. Tom did not yet know his name, but Erick Swan was now acting too calm to be an innocent bystander. Tom followed him.

Erick immediately became aware of Tom following him and broke into a jog toward a large group of attendees as they flooded out of the four glass double doors in the front of the church building being used as the Assembly room. Erick Swan blended into the running crowd and disappeared.

Others were streaming from the many side doors that assembly-type buildings are required to provide for exits. The panicking crowd knocked Tom to the ground, and he covered his head as they ran by him.

Smoke poured from the building and the Military Emergency Services began arriving. Tom was trying to call James to see if he had made it out, but all cell phone services had stopped working as the upgraded system was overwhelmed by thousands of connections at once.

Tom ran into the building's side door as a dazed woman fell through the opening. A smell that Tom had never smelled before filled the room. Tom looked to the back area that James had been occupying but saw nothing but smoke.

"Are you OK?"
"Get out of here. You can't be here."
"Do you need help?"

Three different voices were shouting at Tom and he realized that he should leave and look for James outside. The interior of the building had hundreds of people, some moaning, some laying very still. Tom was not a war veteran and he was not prepared for what he saw.

Erick Swan walked East. His DRAG Systems' bosses, none of whom were citizens of this nation had not been as tolerant of these meetings as Raul had been. Raul's ambitions to have power in the next political landscape of the Middle *Quarters* were not shared by the leaders of DRAG Systems. They were already monitoring 70% of the World's economies.

Erick Swan's plan was to shift the blame for this DRAG Systems assassination to another group. Raul and other *1st Quarter* Media Centers would get credible reports that the KC Workers Party had planted the bomb that killed Roachman (Raul's favorite Kansas politician) and Clark Williamson. Raul would be conflicted – happy that Clark was dead and sad that Arne Nelson would not get Roachman's support and become Raul's man on the inside of *3rd Quarter* politics.

Erick Swan had one other thing to do before he disappeared into central Missouri. He walked one mile to Pomposa's Military Com Center. He entered and caught Captain Pomposa's eye and nodded to the back of the building.

He met Briana behind the makeshift building on the I-35 bypass and whispered, "I got to get out of here." As he leaned in to whisper to Briana, he shoved a knife up and under her flak jacket. He calmly walked away as Briana collapsed.

Two more explosions went off behind him somewhere around the center of Bethany. Erick Swan walked into the adjacent cornfield. The 7-foot corn stalks masking his presence and the red soil staining his white sneakers.

26

Three Months Later

T hey will believe anything that we tell them if we repeat it enough." Denny Flanders was having a rare meeting with Raul and one staff member at his 550-acre estate. Gordon was in the last fully operational hospital in Richmond. Gordon had been attacked by an unknown group of young men, just North of Central City.

Denny continued, "We need to move the Media Center managers back to the Media Centers and get them out of the upper management of the *Right to have a Job Initiative*. They are screwing everything up.

"If we cannot get our message out there, these roving bands of outlaws will continue to disrupt our communities. We just need to educate them about the good or what we are doing."

Raul sat next to the large open fireplace and was getting too warm but didn't move. His staff member was even closer and wasn't complaining either.

Raul knew that it had been Denny's idea to take zealot Media Center personnel and move them into upper management positions of the new *Right to have a Job Initiative*. And it had been a disaster. To start and manage a new program required a slight connection to reality. These zealots had gotten their promotions by making up their own reality. There was mass confusion.

Raul responded, "I will use everyone in the old *Right to Pay* employee archives and move the Media Center people back to where they are most needed." He knew when to avoid pointing the finger of who was at fault. There was a new unspoken rule in the *1ˢᵗ Quarter*.

"When your boss is wrong, don't tell him."

Men and women getting new jobs under the *Right to have a Job Initiative* laughed when they said it. Most days were spent doing something that would be undone the next day. But the pay was good, so everyone quickly conformed to the new rule. Silence paid more.

Raul continued, "I will visit the Media Centers and relay anything you would like them to know about our present predicament. Of Course, we still control the narrative and will continue to repeat whatever is needed." Raul had taken over Gordon and Denny's oversight of the Media Centers since the Federal Government had broken the 3 Agreements, they had with the *1ˢᵗ Quarter.*

Denny Flanders interrupted Raul, "What we really need is to really, really believe in this *Right to have a Job Initiative.* It will work if people… really believe that everyone… should have a job. This great country of ours…. is rich enough that we can easily… make sure each citizen has a job that pays well."

Raul looked at Denny as he rambled on and realized that the old man would probably not make it through the next election cycle at his present rate of mental deterioration. Raul no longer believed in anything that Denny said. Raul was just trying to survive like everyone else.

"Maybe we could give past employees of the *Right to Pay Initiative* a Loyalty Test… Maybe train 100 of our New Morality teachers how to administer a lie detector test and find thousands of LOYAL followers that really, really believe…." Denny's gaze was far off and focused on nothing.

Raul didn't hesitate and nodded with a smile wondering where he was going to find 100 lie detector thing-a-ma-jigs. "I think that is a great idea. But like you say, we must continue to use the Media Centers to educate the public about how wonderful it will be when we have 100% employment. The public just doesn't understand…"

They continued to talk, and Raul began to realize that he was there to give Denny a sounding board for Denny's own ideas and nothing was going to be accomplished – other than wasting Raul's time.

ONE MONTH LATER
NewPOP1 – Tom and James Return

Tom, James, and Janet drove past the group of 5 men beating an older man with a shopping cart. It was harder and harder to find shopping carts. They had become the pedestrian's friend. One of the men looked up and barked, "Keep moving. He keeps calling NewPOP1 'New York' and we can't have this disrespect. He knows – that it is offensive to talk like this."

James and Tom had made it back from Bethany after the chaos of the 3 blasts in Bethany. They were happy to see their friends in the Believers group in NewPOP1.

Janet drove to a new apartment in the unregulated part of the city. They drove into an underground gated garage with a security guard behind bulletproof glass monitoring and controlling the entrance.

Once in the apartment, Janet excitedly asked, "So what happened? We have no news. We are completely in the dark. Our media is saying that a rogue Workers Group in KC had bombed some meeting near 3POP18."

James began, "We came back through the Northern way and it took forever…."

"Honey, let Tom tell us what is happening with the New Federal Government." Janet quietly broke into James's comments.

Tom started, "Well I have good news and I have bad news. The bad news is that we need to move inland as far as we can. There are no more Federal protections of the East Coast. The 3 Agreements that the old Federal government had with the *1st Quarter* are now null."

Janet said, "That is bad news. Have you seen how bad it is out there? It has gotten worse since you left. Civil protections have broken down. And there is another big problem. This came to our old address yesterday for James." Janet handed Tom an official-looking letter from the old *Right to Pay Initiative.*

Tom opened it and saw that James was being offered a senior management position in the *Right to have a Job Initiative.* He would have to pass a Loyalty Test that was included in the letter. It was a questionnaire with 10 questions. If James passed this test, he was guaranteed a job in upper management.

"Oh no," Tom had been ready to move the whole group. Now he would have to reconsider staying to support James. This opportunity for James may help with the cause. "NewPOP1, NewPOP2, and NewPOP3 are not safe. If we are going to stay, let's see if we can at least move away from the center of the city."

Five more of the Believers group arrived and sat in the small room, with the blackout curtains drawn over the large windows.

Janet was impatient, "What's the good news? What happened in Bethany Missouri?"

Tom started a narrative that jumped back and forth in time. The group sat hanging on each of his words as he described what had happened in the last three months.

"It wasn't the KC Workers Group that was responsible for the bombing, it was that guy that is high up in the Richmond *1st Quarter* Administration. I saw him when the first bomb went off... I thought we had lost James." He smiled at James, "But let me start at the beginning."

Three Months Later

What Happened After the Bethany Bombing

Tom told his story to the group. As the story grew to a close, Tom told them what happened after the blast.

"I was an eyewitness. That guy from the *1st* *Quarter* Administration was involved in this bombing. "As James and I traveled back, we contacted many of the Liberty Groups and this is the story that they told us.

"The Ex-Californian used his contacts with the Federal Military and established a video link that had the data capacity to carry over 45 connections. These 45 links were used by the Middle *Quarter's* Liberty Groups and State politicians to continue and complete the work of the Bethany Assembly and the new Bill of Rights.

"Before we left the North country last week, we were informed that 34 States had ratified the New Bill of Rights and Constitution.

"Eleven *2nd* *Quarter* States, fifteen *3rd* *Quarter* States, four independent States that broke from the *4th* *Quarter* and 3 States that broke with the *1st* *Quarter* – 34 States now form the New United States of America.

"This new Constitution's Bill of Rights is not the goofy rights that Denny Flanders promises everyone. They guarantee each citizen the right to be free from the government.

"Those in leadership in the Middle *Quarters* had thought that it would take several years to ratify the new Bill of Rights and the full constitution. But when they killed Clark Williamson, his last speech was distributed and motivated many groups to do something.

"His last words were, 'We are here to save a nation.' This slogan was published in print by the RR's and the video of Clark's last words and his death went viral unedited. The one man that the *1st* *Quarter* was the most afraid of was murdered while calling for the country to agree upon a new Constitution." Tom took a drink of the glass of water someone had just handed him.

Everyone in the room had seen the video. The *1st Quarter* Media Centers had tried to muddy the facts by blaming a Liberty Group that had radically broken from their previous alliances. Other "reporters" said that it had been a rogue military group that wanted to keep the status quo.

The Main Media Center story that was reported was Eric Swan's DRAG Systems cover story of the KC Workers group. The Media Centers had learned long ago that if only one story was reported that no one would believe it. They had released many conflicting stories at the same time.

Those in the room smiled, now knowing the truth and were hopeful for a better future.

Tom continued, "The old Federal Government politicians have been asked to vacate their offices. The Federal Military leadership has recognized the new Government and will soon begin moving assets to the New United States.

"The National Guard will begin to enforce border security. A ten-year moratorium has been declared for all movement between the East and West Borders of the New United States. We have ten years of freedom of movement into and out of the coastal *Quarters*.

"Also, the money supply will be controlled by the New United States immediately, so if you have anything saved spend it now on something that will be valuable – your *1st Quarter* dollars will soon be worthless.

Three Months Later

"The free press of the New United States is guarded by law from government or political manipulations and will soon begin a mass news release with the story that I have just told you.

"I assume the Media Centers will try to release confusing accounts deleting facts that are dangerous to their power positions. But the message will slowly get out to the *1ˢᵗ and 4ᵗʰ Quarters*. When that happens, I am not sure what New POP1 will look like.

"There are stories, from the Northern *4ᵗʰ Quarter* that any group with a strong leader and enough weapons can rule their region. Unelected, well-armed warlords are becoming recognized as legitimate leaders."

More of the Believers group had filtered into the room as Tom was talking and no one had said anything. They were waiting for some type of direction. The desire to flee the East Coast immediately was the group's emotional response to Tom's news.

Janet spoke up, "We should all be prepared to leave quickly when circumstances dictate. But there may be one final job we have here in New POP1. James has been offered a high-level job in the *Right to Have a Job Initiative.*"

David Micah spoke up, "I will help with my contacts in the business community. But the DRAG Systems people are monitoring everyone and aggressively screening business managers now.

Jim Brooks teenage daughter Dakota asked, "Shouldn't we all try to contact our relatives in the Middle... I mean the New United States and tell them that we might be seeing them, sooner than later?"

The group started mingling and eating some food that Hannah had set out as Tom was talking. Someone suggested praying, but everyone was talking about their plans to leave the city and how and when it might happen.

27

The First Federal Election

The New United States - State representatives sat in the Great Room of the Ex-California's home. There were only 2 family cars in his circular front driveway. The SUV's that had brought the 34 State representatives were hidden in his 6-car garage in the rear of his home. Space had been cleared so that these 34 men and women could enjoy a quiet time of discussion.

The Northern Anti-American Barriers 240 miles north had made this location dangerous to some. This house also was only 300 miles West of Old Chicago now known as the *Lawless Lands*. Some attendees were jumpy being so close to those who were now the sworn enemies of all freedoms enjoyed by the New United States' citizens.

"The ratifying States need to submit to Congress in a joint proceeding of the House and the Senate the exact State Boundaries. But before we can do that, we will have to have a Congress to meet." The Ex-California immediately jumped into the first agenda item.

He was standing on the raised hearth of the 16-foot-high open fireplace, in the Great Room. The meeting was informal. Some had old paper tablets open – others their electronic tablets. By agreement, no pictures or videos would be allowed in these meetings. Everyone had agreed to one historian videoing the group meetings. These would be kept in a secure location for the next several years.

These 34 men and women were now scattered from behind the large kitchen island, the breakfast nock, the sunken Great Room and surrounding raised areas. There were no meeting rules since everyone had conducted so many meetings themselves and learned by experience the right and wrong way to have a meeting.

The First Federal Election

The Ex-Californian continued, "So, I am not sure how you would like to do this, but I would suggest that we divide into groups of 4 or 5 and discuss the following." A screen lowered in the area above his head and glowed with a list of three bullet points from the projector above.

1. Who should vote in the first Federal Election?
2. How should we vote in the first Federal Election?
3. When and how will the vote be verified and reported?

"It is up to each State to determine the answer to these three questions under the new Bill of Rights and the new Constitution. I have prepared each of you a copy. But as you know this document was intentionally minimal allowing for each State to establish their own rules."

The Ex-Californian clicked a small device and the screen above his head changed. "I have included an expanded list on the hard copies you are now being given." The Ex-Californian's wife, Michelle began handing copies out - 5 at a time and each person in the group passed the copy on to the person closest to them.

1. Who should vote in the first Federal Election?
    A. Length of time of residency.
    B. How citizens will prove their residency.
    C. How to treat new arrivals.
    D. Since there has been no count – how should the House numbers be determined - new census or estimates?

2. How should we vote in the first Federal Election?
    A. What regulations should be instituted in each State?
    B. How should a two-party system be encouraged by the States?
    C. How should the New Morality Party be treated?

3. When and how will the vote be verified and reported?

The Ex-Californian continued, "The only way that we will succeed with this New United States is with the backing of the citizens. If we run elections the way the *1st Quarter* has run their elections, we will lose any credibility with the general population."

A man who looked to be in his forties spoke up. "We must have a government of the people, by the people and for the people…."

A younger woman next to him spoke, "That's right, to rule we must represent the will of the people while guaranteeing the liberty of each citizen in our nation."

Richards's personal assistant, Esther stood to address the group. Her wisdom and personal respect for those in the room had given her a special place of influence throughout the New United States. "Tomorrow morning, I would like each of us to introduce ourselves to the group and take one or two minutes addressing the group.

"I would ask you to relay one message that Richards will be releasing throughout the *2nd Quarter* and the *3rd Quarter*.

"First, we are now calling the States that have ratified the new Constitution the New United States. We will no longer be using the terms *2nd and 3rd Quarter,* in all our communications. After decades the man on the street may continue to use whatever names he likes, but we want to make a quick and firm change that will redefine who we are.

"Second, Richards is not going to run for any office, and he will not be appearing in any of these or other meetings. He wants to help but not be the focus.

"Lastly, as we all choose new Representatives for the Federal positions, let us stress the positions as servant positions. We are not electing rulers – we are electing servants. Men and women who want to serve for one term. All terms are one-term with no return to any Federal Position after the one term, per the new Constitution.

The Ex-Californian stood and continued, "Please do not go into the front yard area. You can roam around in the back area as you wish. There are tables set up back there.

"This new Federal Government and the new State Governments also will be restricted in their powers. The States, the counties and the cities within will not be looking to the Federal Government to fix their problems.

"I know most of you are familiar with the new constitution. But I am not sure if we are prepared for the stupidity that we are about to hear, as ambition men try to gain power. These same men ruined our country with their lies and hidden agendas. They are about to come out of the shadows again. Some already hold positions in the Middle *Quarters* Administrations.

"Let us find selfless men and women who will serve and then return to non-government positions. Let us find men and women who will not try to profit from their service but sacrifice to serve."

28

The Right to Have a Job

The *Right to have a Job Initiative* was being implemented using the old – now-defunct *Right to Pay* structure. The nightly riots and civil unrest had calmed as the masses in the *1st Quarter* looked to the government once again for hope.

The present *1st Quarter* Administration under Denny Flanders had stated in word, if not in actions that everyone living under their rule had the right to:

1. Housing
2. Food
3. Healthcare
4. Transportation
5. A Living Wage Job

Tom, James, and Janet had decided to stay one more year in the *1st Quarter* and support James since he was one of the regional managers of the *Right to have a Job Initiative*. Most of the Believers group had relocated to the outer edges of New POP1 but had also stayed.

James had passed the Loyalty Test, with the help of Janet and Tom. James had problems comprehending certain questions. He also did not like lying about his beliefs. Tom had explained that James was being given a great opportunity to serve fellow Believers, by reporting back to him and the group what was happening.

Tom had little hope that James could succeed and worried that James may be exposed by the Morality Warriors. There were stories every day of gangs of men attacking someone. Since all healthcare was run by the *1st Quarter* Administration, emergency services were overwhelmed and only responded to specific "safe" neighborhoods.

The Right to Have a Job

James had been on the job 45 days and was now in charge of 5 Districts. After his 3 weeks of training, James had risen quickly due to his ability to shut up and not have an opinion.

James had learned this skill in High School. He had found that most of the time if he did not say anything, everyone assumed he understood what was happening.

Now James seemed to have the perfect job. The more he simply smiled and nodded, occasionally repeating back what the speaker was saying, James was accepted as a good manager.

James was visiting local businesses and had asked Tom to accompany him. He had been given a vehicle and a new residence where the other managers lived. James drove to Tom's parking garage. Tom didn't actually live here, but only Hannah knew this.

James asked Tom to drive. James didn't like to drive – too many quick decisions to make. "Drive up Parkway 4 and stop at…" James gave Tom the address.

James explained to Tom what he was going to be doing all day. "It is my job to simply walk in, count how many people are working, take a picture of the workforce and text it to my assistant." They drove by the Jumbovision with Denny Flanders speaking about the *5 Rights* of every citizen.

Denny's words boomed out from the video. "… loving administration is concerned about the plight of all who live …"

Tom thought, "The plight of living with Denny Flanders trying to solve the world's problems with money he no longer has…"

James and Tom walked into Agro Chemical. James identified himself as being the new Director of the *Right to have a Job Initiative.* 135 employees were lined up and photographed in 5 large groups. James sent his assistant the 5 pictures on his phone. 25 seconds later James received his assistant's text.

"14 new employees – next Wednesday."

"Next week, I will be sending 14 new employees for you to hire. You will be required to guarantee a living wage for two years to these 14 employees." The young receptionist, a bearded 20 something man named Cole looked at James like he was from another planet.

"Let me call my…."

James cut him off. "I have to leave now. If you would like to talk with someone further, about this here is my card. Or you can go to our website and find the information there."

James left quickly – the program had found that it was good to leave quickly after making these "requests" of businesses.

"So, what happens if they call the number on your card?" Tom asked.

"They will be directed to the *Right to have a Job Initiative's* website. I am not sure what is on it, because the few times I have gone there, I got lost on a page that finally timed out."

Tom grimaced. He knew the procedure. "What if they stay on the line and try to ask a human a question?"

James looked at him thinking. "The number is the number of a phone in the back of my office. I had my assistant unplug it. The ringing was really starting to disrupt the productivity of the office."

James had learned several words that he now incorporated into normal conversations throughout the day. "Productivity" was his favorite new word.

James continued, "I think they are sending me someone to answer the phone, but I don't know…" James abruptly stopped as Tom swerved to avoid a small group of men with masks over their faces.

"Damn Morality Warriors, should stay out the street," Tom muttered under his breath. They pulled up to AAE and stopped. Tom used to buy the products of this brand when they were American Auto Equipment. With the Purity Purges, all business names were changed to acronyms. If it was good enough for AT&T, everyone else can do it too. The business would have lost its license to employ if it had kept the "American" – too offensive.

Tom and James walked into AAE and James identified himself as the new District Director of the *Right to have a Job Initiative*. James took 10 pictures of 96 employees as he walked the factory floor. Texted them to his assistant. The text came back.

"10 new employees next Monday"

The factory floor had been spread out and Tom thought he saw a bunch of people running out the back door as they entered the factory. James hadn't been quick enough this time to escape without talking to a person in charge. The owner showed up as he was making his announcement in the lobby of AAE.

"What do you mean 10 new employees? What is the current living wage? By who's authority are you doing this?" The owner was red-faced and probably had high blood pressure before James's visit.

James handed the owner of AAE his card. "Call this number or go to the *Right to have a Job Initiative* website, please. I am only here to evaluate how many employees you will be required to employ. We thank you for being a responsible business owner who cares about the community you serve."

James had been taught this exact line. It had taken him two days and he still did not know what it meant. Neither did anyone else. But it sure sounded good.

Tom was back in the car with James. "So besides visiting employers, what else do you do for the initiative? Do you ever see the raw numbers for your district?"

James spoke slowly, "I only have two other jobs. One is to address those in the 5 District Offices each month." James had learned to keep his pep talks short and to the point. He used phrases he had been taught in Upper Management training.

> This is a win-win situation.
> We are not in a zero-sum game here.
> We should get all our ducks in a row.
> I want to touch base offline with each of you.
> I wanted to give you all a heads up on this.
> We need to run that up the flagpole again.

James continued, "The second thing that I have to do is oversee our In-House Jobs Programs. Each district has several, I am not sure how many. I visit them and see how they are doing."

"And how are they doing?" asked Tom.

"Well, the employees seem to be pretty happy. They sit at terminals and read or eat or something. I got a memo that the terminals were going to be connected in the next 60 days."

Tom drove to the next stop of the day. A company renamed FU2. This used to be Fairchild Unified and it was run by a rebel that did not believe in the New Morality or the 2 Commands of Love. Tom pulled up and stopped before an old factory with bars on the windows and doors. It looked like it was closed.

"So, what do the In-House employees do at their terminals once the terminals are turned on?"

James glanced at the **OUT of BUSINESS** sign on the front door of FU2 and quickly said, "I don't know."

Tom drove around to a fenced parking lot that was also deteriorating and saw at least 250 cars of all ages and models. "Are you sure that this factory still has a license to operate in New POP2?" Then Tom saw it. A small dirty side door that had handprints all over it.

Tom and James entered this door and immediately heard loud factory equipment. All the windows were painted black on the inside and there was an armed guard at the entrance.

They were immediately greeted by Frank Fairchild a crusty half bearded man. "I am the owner here. What do you want?"

James started into his regular routine and tried to walk onto the factory floor. He was immediately stopped by the guard.

"I said, what do you want?" Frank was louder this time. As James started into his routine again, Frank interrupted him. "I want you to leave, NOW."

Frank Fairchild was now yelling. "I don't know who you are or who you think you are, but if I have any trouble of any kind, in the next months, I will find you and I will hurt you. You understand!"

James just stared at him. Tom waited 6 seconds for James to respond and then answered for James. "No problem, we will remove you from our list of businesses participating in the *Right to have a Job Initiative*. No problem. We don't want any trouble from you or anyone else."

Tom ushered James out the small side door as James was still trying to understand what had just happened.

Tom drove off quickly. "James it is places like that, that may be our friends. If there is any hope for the East Coast, we have to find those who will fight back."

"From now on when you find a place that refuses to cooperate, I want you to do two things. Don't write this down." James had reached for a small tablet.

"ONE – mark that business as out of business in your district and TWO – report their name and address to Janet. No texts, no phone calls, no voice mails, just report in person to Janet at the end of the day. Understand?"

James nodded. Tom drove to the final stop of the day. The sign FSI was still high on the front. The windows were broken out and it looked like there were smoke stains along one side.

The owner or manager or employees of FSI had spray-painted across the front in large letters their final statement.

WE ARE No LONGER in BUSINESS
DuE TO THE RIGHT TO a JOB AND LIVING WAGe

Tom read the sign out loud and said, "What did your bosses tell you to do when this happens?" James didn't know. Tom asked him to report back to Janet anytime this happens. No texting, no phone calls, no voice mails, just in-person reporting back to Janet.

James and Tom had a meeting with the Believers Group in the afternoon, once his runs were done. There was too much exposure for the group to meet in James's new upscale house in the gated manager's community. So, they met in James's old apartment. The apartment manager's office had been closed and there was no one to give the keys back to, so James kept them.

Tom drove to James's old apartment in the unmonitored section of New POP1. There the group met for prayer. Nothing of the day's events were discussed with the group. This small time of meeting with friends was what James needed to continue to function in his job as District Manager.

Tom and Janet dismissed themselves from the 12 people present and Tom asked Janet to report James's data to him. It could be very valuable to extrapolate the data for the populated areas of the East Coast. Also, James was in a perfect position to find friends of freedom that could help with the fight.

Tom had two final requests.

ONE: Tom would like to accompany James on his field trips for the next couple of weeks.

TWO: Could James employ one of the members of the group in his District Office of the *Right to have a Job Initiative*?

After eating together, the group left one or two at a time before the 10 p.m. curfew in New POP1.

29

The FU2 Media Hacks

Tom pulled up to the Fairchild Unified Factory the next week to talk with Frank Fairchild privately. "I have some very, very valuable news for you and your business." After Tom explained his present job for Charter Bank and his travels in the Middle *Quarters*, Frank wanted to know more.

"The reason I am coming to you is because you make some of the components in the large Jumbovision screens we see on New POP buildings. Could you access these from a remote location?" Tom asked.

"Why would I want to do that? Of course, the streams that feed the Jumbovision have hardware that might have a back door for upgrades to the software. But again, why would I want to do that?" Frank was still skeptical of who Tom was.

Tom lowered his voice for emphasis and said, "I would like to make a proposal to you. It is worth all the money you presently have saved and any assets you hold in the *1ˢᵗ Quarter*."

Tom's statement made Frank want to know more. But Frank was a poker player and he had his poker face on. "I doubt that. But please continue." Frank called Tom's hand. He wanted to see what Tom had.

"I would like to hack every Jumbovision or other devices that your components power in a random fashion for a 7-day period starting this July 4ᵗʰ.

"Since Richards's hack, security has really tightened. In exchange for helping me, I will give you insider information on the biggest event to happen to the *1st Quarter* since the Purity Purges."

Frank was not a Believer and he didn't even own the Book, but he had been taught a valuable lesson by his father, Frank Sr. *Never Underestimate the Power of Very Stupid People in Large Groups.* He had a sign stating that sentiment directly behind his desk. Tom was looking at it now and it gave Tom hope, that Frank would help.

"If you can deliver on what you are saying, I can deliver on what you want," Frank responded.

Tom continued, "On July 4th there are going to be Drone Drops and other media hacks to announce that there is a New United States. The U.S. dollars that are now being used in the *1st Quarter* will quickly dry up as the New United States takes control of the money supply.

"The Military has already begun moving its assets out of the *1st and 4th Quarters*. 34 states have already ratified a new Constitution and a new Bill of Rights."

Tom could not give him a copy but the New Bill of Rights because they were being held for the announcements. But Tom could tell him some of the changes.

He continued, "The new Bill of Rights is based upon the Right to be left alone. The Federal Government and the States, Counties and Cities will be restricted in their ability to Tax, Regulate or intrude. Judges will have limited terms.

"There will be no more career politicians. One Term and no more Federal Service will be mandated by the constitution and Civil Servants will be held accountable for their actions as servants of the people."

Tom pointed to the sign behind Frank's head, "Stupid people in large groups will no longer have the power to make laws that suit their fancy and then enforce them with no limitations. All New Morality stupidity will be seen as what it is – Tyranny of the Majority."

Frank Fairchild's eyes were wide and if Frank could express excitement, his face was giving his emotions away, just a little. "I'm in!"

Tom continued, "This is valuable and dangerous information. The *1st Quarter* Administration already knows some of this information and they must be aware of the Military's moves. If they think you have the up-to-date information you will be put in a secure New Morality Training Center. Your family may never see you again.

"I will send someone to get your help with the hacking. I will never come back to this building. NEW U.S. is our trust word. If anyone says they have been sent by me, don't ask them for the trust word. Let them volunteer NEW U.S. If they don't, they cannot be trusted, and you should assume you have been compromised."

Frank, half-shaved face and gruff manner was now thinking about where to move his family and to whom to sell his assets. Someone who loved Denny Flanders and his nonsense.

June 1 – Federal Election Day

Craig Carmichael, Richards and the Ex-Californian were sitting in a small room somewhere in Free Colorado, south of I-70. This room was built into the side of a mountain and had hardened landlines on an old N-Carrier transmission system.

These hardened lines had been wired into Military bases throughout the nation so communications could be maintained no matter what was happening outside the mountain. E-pulse or atmospheric atomic blasts could not disrupt these old N-Carrier communications. The equipment frames were mounted on raised heavy-duty springs in case the ground started shaking.

The *4th Quarter* and *1st Quarter* connections to these Military lines had been literally cut, before the Bethany Assembly. Now Craig Carmichael, (minus one eye due to Erick Swan's bomb) sat watching the real-time election results of the first federal elections of the New United States.

Craig Carmichael had run for the first Senate seat of North Texas. Everyone who was injured in Erick Swan's bomb had been elevated to celebrity status in their regions. A few imposters had been promoted by the KC Star, but the DD daily had identified the posers as not even attending the Bethany Assembly meetings.

The Des Moines Register had started using their name again and had terminated all reporters and editors and replaced them with the ambitious 30 somethings that had been reporting for the DD Daily, throughout the middle States. These young reporters detested the lazy journalists that got their stories from other news releases. They were careful to be truthful.

The Register was now a part of the daily Drone Drops that had run most of the newspapers of the middle States out of business. It took money to produce a newspaper and you can only lie to people for so long until they stop buying the lie. Most businesses watched the takeover of the economy under DRAG Systems and stopped advertising.

Now, these three men would watch the election results together. Other Bethany Assembly attendees and other politicians also watched in secure locations. These same hardened lines would transmit the State results as they were certified under State Rules.

The first result was in from East Kansas. Arne Nelson would be a Representatives from the KCK region. Arne had lost an arm in the Bethany blast and no one opposed his candidacy. Raul's undercover friend was tall and had a way about him. He seemed to be concerned for everyone. In reality, Arne was just a tall, good looking airhead with a nice smile.

The Register had started a campaign to rename the New United States elected officials to Servants and/or Ministers. The DD Daily had started calling politicians "The Elected" or "The Unelected." The idea of politicians or even public servants was repugnant to many who had endured the corruption and regulations of men who acted as if they were morally superior to the electorate.

The first Congress would meet in Independence Missouri. Each State would donate one Federal building to house Federal Elected officials to start this fragile second attempt of citizen self-rule.

As the evening progressed, the decentralization of the Federal elections helped keep Morality Warriors' skirmishes to a minimum. The National Guard had been at full strength along the border States.

By the end of the night, the government of the New United States was elected, and many States did not wait to swear in their representatives. By 2 a.m. over 80% of the Elected had sworn to uphold the following:

1. Represent their electorate
2. To maintain freedom and liberty in all their actions
3. To conform to and uphold the New Bill of Rights
4. To not lie or hide information from the public

The electoral college would meet on July 3rd to swear in the first President of the New United States. July 4th would again become a time of celebration at least in half the country.

30

The July 4th Celebrations

It was July 1st and small flyers and booklets dropped from the sky. Old Florida, Georgia, Carolinas, and the border states were targeted on July 1st. The booklets were small and were produced by *Youth for Good Democracy.*

L – A – R – S

Limited

Accountable

Restrained

Servants

**Good Democracy
Can Only be Practiced with
Safeguards against Tyranny**

The pamphlets were rough but got their point across. To have Good Democracy, the Majority should not have the ability to vote for anything they want. That is the Tyranny of the Majority.

Law should be limited to the protection of citizens and property.

All laws should be well defined and reviewed.

Reset can only happen with Term Limits.

Someone's Freedom is limited by every law.

The flyers fell on the final caravans of military vehicles as they drove west, south, and east and relocated to within the New United States' borders.

There had been strategic movements ordered 60 days earlier, so this final move would look less dramatic. Civilians and dependent families had been moved to the 2nd and 3rd Quarters. But now the Final Orders had been issued to all East and West Coast military bases 6 a.m. July 1st. No explanation was given to the Commanders of why these orders were given.

The Final Order

This material may not be published, broadcast, rewritten or redistributed – No cell phone contact or other communications will be allowed until you arrive at your destination.

Move all assets to the Base described in A33 Doc.
Leave immediately with no communication to anyone.
Leave all facilities as is.

New Advance Bases had been set up inside the new State borders that had been defined by the New United States. Thirty days earlier the National Guard had been assigned to the problem border areas.

July 2nd

FU2 techs were making their final updates to the software at the hardwired locations on all Jumbovision large screens. These locations controlled hundreds of video feeds throughout the 1st Quarter.

Frank Fairchild had already sold his company to one of his gated community neighbors who loved Denny Flanders and his Administration. Since there were no buyers of residential real estate in the 1st Quarter, Frank traded his 6500 square foot house for real property that was loaded on two cargo trucks.

Frank had been contacted by a young college girl from *Youth for Good Democracy* with the code word, New U.S. She had given him 3 separate video clips to upload to the Jumbovision systems.

Other *Youth for Good Democracy* college students had given the same 3 video clips to insiders at Print and Broadcast Media outlets throughout the communities of the *1ˢᵗ Quarter*.

The DD Daily print shop locations had been given one final News Release for July 5ᵗʰ - the name of the New United States President.

July 3ʳᵈ

240 Electoral college electors met in Independence Missouri and cast their votes for the first President of the New United States. There had been three candidates on the 34 State ballots.

The Workers Party
The New Morality Party
The Liberty Party

The men running in all three parties had limited name recognition. The new State election boards wanted to error on the side of honest wording. Each State had adopted slightly different guidelines to communicate each Political Party's position. The new Constitution restricted each State to the old *Winner Take All* electoral college process.

The Parties were not allowed to put their own wording on the ballot. After the *4ᵗʰ Quarter's* Old California deception and out-right lying on official ballots, no party was allowed to distort their message on the official ballot.

Specific words had been banned from Ballot language due to the corruption of the language by the Media Centers for the past decade. The goal was to communicate facts ONLY. No hyperbole or other forms of distortion were allowed.

Richards's name was a "Write-In" and won with 85% of the vote. He carried every State by over 30 points. No one knew where Richards was, but the announcement would be made anyway.

Tom still in New POP1 received a call from his contact at *Youth for Good Democracy,* "We don't know Richards's first name! Or is Richards his first name and we don't know his last name?" The young girl seemed under a lot of stress.

"His full name is Terry R. Richards with the middle initial standing for Rick. So maybe, just use the R." Tom responded. He quickly flashed on a scenario where the announcement was made, and he found out he had been mistaken. But he was 99% sure he was correct. "Go with Terry R. Richards in your DD Daily for tomorrow."

The 4th of July 5 a.m.

State Governments did not have enough money to buy fireworks for the 4th of July Celebrations. The New Federal Government had no money at all. But many municipalities issued a call to any individual or business that wanted to organize fireworks displays throughout the old *2nd and 3rd Quarters.*

Every city, town and small community gathered to celebrate freedom. Some celebrations were organized by Liberty Groups, but most were simple expressions of excitement for the new opportunities a free country provided to them and their children.

5 a.m. July 4th Terry Richards landed at a private airfield and drove 50 miles to Independence Missouri. The cameras were set up and the newly sworn-in Justices of the Supreme Federal Court stood in a line. There was no Chief Justice. 5 men and 4 women stood before Richards.

Richards looked down at a piece of paper he had written one hour ago.

"I, Terrance Rick Richards solemnly affirm that I will,

"With the help of God,

"Faithfully maintain and guard the liberties that this Constitution guarantees each individual citizen of these New United States.

"And I will execute my duties as President of these New United States without deceit, with a clear understanding of the principles of limited government.

"As God is my witness."

There were only a few in attendance, but cameras were catching this moment. Richards looked up and smiled at the 9 men and women standing with him on this small raised platform. He reached out and shook each hand with a comment to each.

"Let's do it right this time.
"You stay in your lane and I assure you I will stay in my lane.
"I pray that you define the constitution with our original intent.
"Please pray for me, as I execute the new laws.
"May we each uphold the principles of liberty in this document."

These men and women were keenly aware that this would probably be the last chance for citizen's self-rule with most of the world under some type of financial or social tyranny.

Each shook one another's hand and then also responded to Richards's exhortations. The atmosphere was sober but informal on this soberest of occasions.

The RR Daily and Social Media were flooded with reports, videos and news releases by 6 in the morning. Military communication channels carried the video of this event with commentary by Ja'Ron Stuart representing the Des Moines Register and Craig Carmichael representing the Federal Government of the New United States.

Ja'Ron's tone was serious as he asked Craig Carmichael clarifying questions about what this meant for the citizens of the 34 States of the New United States.

They talked about what happened at the Bethany Assembly. They discussed the eye-witness account of a *1st Quarter* operative quickly leaving the area immediately after the blast that had killed 24 and seriously wounded 56 men and women.

The producer of this Media Event piece signaled to wrap it up and within minutes this Video Clip was playing on all National Guard and Military Com-lines across the world.

4th of July 10 a.m.

Starting exactly at 10 a.m. the same video began to randomly play throughout the Jumbovision and smaller screens of the *1st Quarter*. Instead of people walking past and ignoring the grinning face of Denny Flanders, telling everyone how virtuous he was, people stopped and stared. Crowds began to form to listen to real news.

4th of July 11 a.m.

At 11 a.m. the *1st Quarter* Media Centers received News Releases from print media reporters in the middle of the country. The Register's News Release was the most detailed and carried names, times and places. The Media Centers did not release any of these reports.

By noon the phones in the Media Centers were ringing from other reporters, pseudo reporters and talking heads that had to respond to the developing news stories with something. Since the official news had not released, most news outlets had nothing to report.

By 12:30 the Media Centers of the *1st Quarter* were up and running, and senior supervisors were getting reports that there had been unauthorized news on the Public Access Channels. Techs were called to investigate the source of the unauthorized news stories.

The July 4th Celebrations

4th of July 1 p.m.

By 1 p.m. the Drone Drops began to drop the full print story of Richards being elected as the President of the New United States and the details surrounding the New Federal Government.

Youth for Good Democracy college students were roving through the streets acting confused but talking with the general public on hidden cameras.

"What does this mean? Does the Army no longer protect the *1st Quarter*?

"You know I saw some Jeeps and large trucks moving the Army tanks yesterday in New POP3."

"We'll ask our professors tomorrow. They must know."

"Maybe this is a good thing. I wonder what those middle country yokels have done this time?"

When the *Youth for Good Democracy* students felt they had enough comments from the general public, they moved on quickly before the masked Morality Warriors showed up.

4th of July 4 p.m.

By 4 p.m. a special curfew had been called in all cities of the *1st Quarter*. Morality Warriors roamed the streets in trucks and cars looking for anyone who may be crowded around the Public Assess screens, large or small.

The public had been driven into their homes where the underground internet was on fire with one Media Center misinformation report after another and hacks of real news.

4th of July 6 p.m.

By 6 p.m. the New United States communities began firing off illegal and legal fireworks across the 34 States. It was not dark yet so most of the fireworks were not seen in the sky, but everyone heard them.

The Media Center pseudo reporters in the *1st Quarter* border cities were the first to call in their observations. Slowly and timidly the real facts were relayed to the Media Centers.

The border cities like Pittsburg had small riots that were stopped by the National Guard. The residents of many border communities began to panic. They had enjoyed living close to the Free Markets of the Middle *Quarters* and its access to products and services at a fair price. But they still owned property in the *1st Quarter* or the Independent Lawless areas.

4th of July 10 p.m.

Sometime after 10 p.m. rockets were fired over the Anti-American Wall that was now called the I-94 wall. It ran roughly between Lake Erie (renamed Hauzu'l-Kausar - the Lake of Abundance) to Lake Michigan (renamed As-Sirāt) along Interstate Highway I-94. I-94 and I-90 were no longer transportation routes, only defining lines between two ideologies.

Since the no-man's-land between I-90 and I-94 was no longer inhabited, this first attack on the New United States did not harm anyone and caused little property damage. The Anti-American militias had already violently killed and beheaded anyone found between I-90 and I-94 several years ago.

The *2nd Quarter* had stationed troops south of I-90 since most of old Michigan had been executing any Believer caught with the Book. Transmissions from this area had been blocked by the Anti-American drone strikes on any perceived cell transmission towers.

The July 4th Celebrations

The Northern Indiana Army Command Center asked for instructions on how to proceed. But the New Federal Government Command structure had not been defined. Everyone was on their own to do what they thought best.

Richards and his team did not hear about this Northern Attack from the closest enemy of the New United States until July 5th. The troops stationed South of I-90, held in position and took no action against the launching of the Anti-American rockets.

July 5th

The Celebrations continued throughout the old *2nd and 3rd Quarters*. Although July 5th was a Saturday everyone had come to work. There was much political talk about what the new Bill of Rights meant for everyone.

Everyone was in a celebratory mood. They had brought cakes decorated with varying wording.

Congrats President Richards
Happy Birthday to the New United States

Many people planned on celebrating throughout the weekend and home parties were planned for Saturday and Sunday. Employers and employees did little work as customers came and went, mainly to talk about the unique time of history that they were witnessing.

31

Connor Quinton Breaks New York

The leaflets were all over the ground in front of James's District Office of *Right to have a Job Initiative*. James was now stationed at the largest District Office in an abandoned factory. His work of assigning new jobs to job seekers had been noticed by upper management and he had been promoted to a desk job – a job that he knew nothing about.

> ***They Promise Us Heaven***
> ***And***
> ***Give Us Hell***

James parked his car in the closest of the three large parking lots that two years ago had held hundreds of factory worker's cars each day. James was happy. The Believers Group had helped him get Hannah, one of the Believers hired as his assistant. Hannah was younger than him, but a great help with interoffice relations.

The other two parking lots were empty except for the line of campers, cars, and motorhomes lining the back fenced area. New POP1 had stopped enforcing all trespass laws and most larger parking lots had lines of people living in their cars, vans or campers. There was a new saying going around New POP1.

Denny's Right to have a camper in a parking lot.

James picked up one of the flyers, that was blowing across the entrance sidewalk to the District Office. On one side he read –

Connor Quinton Breaks New York

Connor Quin Daily

On the other side was the headline of the day. "They Promise us Heaven and Give us Hell." The one-page article detailed the many promises of the 1st *Quarter* Administration, in simple bullet points.

Next, the article detailed the true facts of the condition of employment, housing and general wellbeing of those who still lived in New POP1. James read it quickly and then looked around to see if anyone had seen him pick one up.

This District Office of the *Right to have a Job Initiative* had started assigning workers to come to this factory floor each day. As private employment moved out of the 1st *Quarter*, the initiative had created public sector jobs at an ever-increasing rate. But not fast enough to meet the demand.

As James entered the side entrance, he quickly realized everything was not as it should be. Tables and chairs were overturned in the hallway.

He moved slowly toward his office but stopped as he saw a large group of men and women rummaging through the offices on the far side of the main lobby. The main lobby was three stories high, with a large crystal chandelier hanging in the middle of the lobby. There were several secretaries and the *Right to have a Job Initiative* personnel laying on the lobby floor moaning. Some were lifeless.

James did not know what to do. But had been given an Administration cell phone – one that worked most of the time. He stood in a recessed doorway of a fellow manager and called Tom.

"They're hitting people and – I don't know... I don't know where Hannah is." James was not making any sense. He was concerned for his assistant and fellow Believer Hannah who should be in an office immediately above his head.

"Wait. Calm down. What is happening." Tom said in a low slow voice.

"The workers are attacking people – here – and I am unarmed. What should I do?" James continued. Tom's remarks had not registered.

Tom had heard that many of the job staging areas had lost control of the mass of people looking for work when the jobs that Denny Flanders had promised had not materialized.

There were rumors that most workers in the *Right to have a Job Initiative* were no longer being paid in dollars. Vouchers that were redeemable in Administration Stores were the only payment people were receiving.

James and other District Office personnel had been told to make an announcement that the *1st Quarter* Administration was making changes to the Pay Structure to streamline processes to help the environment.

James had faithfully reported back to Tom that most workers now only had to show up, clock in and sit for their shift's assigned hours. Last week they were no longer required to clock out at the end of the shift. But they would receive a "check" each week in the mail.

Tom could hear in the background from James's cell phone, men shouting. "They promise us Heaven… get Hell…" Tom spoke quickly and urgently to James. "Go up the closest back staircase to the third floor and find Hannah. Then get out of the building and I will meet you at your house in 20 minutes. Call me if you can't find Hannah and I will come and get you."

Tom had feared for James's safety since he had heard the rumors of the new voucher system. Now the workers were rising up and telling Denny Flanders what they thought of his *Right to have a Job Initiative*.

James found Hannah hiding in the back closet of his office on the third floor and they made their way down another back staircase. They could still hear yelling and sounds of destruction as the mob made their way through the corporate offices of upper management.

As James approached his car in the first parking lot, Hannah was leading the way. James looked confused and had not yet processed what was happening. They became a part of the parking lot camper crowd as they yelled and pointed at the smoke now rising in the back of the corporate offices.

James could hear sirens in the distance and sat in the driver's seat not starting his car, just staring. Hannah after 90 seconds looked up at James and whispered, "Let me drive." James just stared at her. She jumped out and quickly drove out of the parking lot before emergency services arrived.

James sat in the passenger's seat trying to remember if he had left anything important in his office. He remembered that he had not signed last week's shift time printouts – the workers would not be paid.

Hannah drove past small mobs of mostly young men, yelling the newest slogan, "They promised us Heaven…."

"Damn Connor Quinton. I wish he had not distributed his Daily Flyer until later in the day after I had gone home." Hannah softly spoke under her breath. She wished she was not in James's newer model car. She drove faster.

As Hannah drove into the gated community where James lived, the armed guard recognized James and gave permission to enter as he opened the cast-iron gate. The security guard looked nervous and as Hannah drove past the small guard shack, she saw two more guards, also looking nervous crouched down.

Tom met them and explained to Hannah, "We are in the perfect storm and we need to find shelter. Pack up and we will meet at Option Z's Western point."

Hannah and James had just witnessed the beginning of the breakdown of the civil authority in New POP1. The group was leaving the *1st Quarter* for good. Hannah started shaking, as James stared at her.

Tom said, "Don't worry. It's just adrenaline." He looked at James who seemed very upset seeing Hannah start to shake.

Tom continued, "Connor Quinton's Daily Flyer has aligned with the *Right to have a Job Initiative's* announcements of changes to the Pay Structure and the first non-dollar Paycheck Vouchers being issued. These events have aligned to start a perfect storm. Let's try to get out of here in one hour or less. James, give me your phone."

Tom texted one sentence to everyone in the Believers Group. *Op-Z – Western Point.*

Richmond – 3 Top Administrators

Raul, Denny, and Gordon were sitting looking out at the green rolling hills that surrounded the 550-acre estate that had been appropriated from the QTZ Corporation when they resisted the New Morality Purges ten years ago.

Now the perimeter roads to this estate were guarded with loyal New Morality soldiers since the military moved out of the *1st Quarter*.

Each man's assistant had been invited to this series of meetings with the three elected Administrators. Decisions had to be made about the condition of the *1st Quarter*. The news was not good. As Raul's assistant spoke softly to him, he spoke up first.

"Is Connor Quinton real? Is he a real person? Or just made up to say stupid things to the uneducated masses. We got a handle on the Drone Drops in large populated areas by shooting them down. But now, somehow the Connor Quin Daily is being distributed in a wider area than ever."

Gordon spoke next, "I think, although no one is admitting it, that people who like the Daily are instructed to pick up packs and just unbundle and leave them in public places..."

Denny Flanders butted in and Gordon shut up. Denny still had more friends and the Morality Warriors on his side and when Denny talked everyone listened. "We have bigger problems than Connor Quinton, whoever he is."

"Next week there will be no more dollars distributed by the Administration. We have started a voucher system for basic necessities. In the larger POP areas, we are giving our friendly supermarkets the exclusive right to accept our vouchers." Denny stopped for dramatic effect.

"BUT these supermarkets do not span all the communities in the *1st Quarter*. And with the rioting in the North, we have no one to set up *Basic Necessity Stores*, as we're calling them."

Softly so as not to be confrontational Raul asked, "When did we start these *Basic Necessity Stores*?" His voice trailing off.

Denny continued, looking annoyed, "I started this program with the authority given to me by the *Right to have a Job Initiative*. We needed jobs and the public needed stores that accept my vouchers."

Gordon, trying to make Denny feel that he was still in control, said, "That sounds like a really good idea. Killing two birds with one stone."

Denny shouted, "YOU idiot. You know that you can't use that phrase since the last Purity Purge. It is very offensive to Bird Lovers everywhere. We have a belief system that has little wiggle room. You say that again, I will bring you up on Morality charges, myself."

At that moment Raul decided that he was going to get out of these meetings as soon as possible and find a safe place. Denny may be a true believer in the New Morality, but he was also an old fool.

Raul spoke quietly, "How are the *Basic Necessity Stores* doing in the smaller communities?" Asking no one in particular in the awkward silence following Denny's outburst.

After what seemed like a long time, Denny's assistant spoke up. "Shipments going to the stores - everything south of 1POP24 (old Charlotte NC) has disappeared. We assume either stolen by the carriers or others. We have taken the Disney Bear off the side of the trucks – we think that is how they were identifying the *Basic Necessity Store* trucks."

"I want the Media Person who came up with the Disney Bear Slogan and logo to be fired from his or her Job. That was the problem. If they just hadn't used that stupid looking Bear to promote the *Basic Necessity Stores.*" Denny was yelling and looked a little unhinged. But everyone smiled and nodded their heads.

Raul sat there and thought, "Shi…. we are doomed. He's more than an old fool. He is crazy." But Raul nodded too.

Gordon's assistant looked at his phone and whispered something to Gordon. Gordon hesitated and then made a calculated decision that it was better to say something than nothing. He jumped up and yelled, "We need to see Public Channel 3. Now!"

Denny Flanders, unaccustomed to Gordon speaking forcefully about anything, which was the only thing that Denny liked about Gordon, looked up and nodded to turn on the TV and tune it to Public 3.

The scene on the screen was rioting and large fires. The announcer was out of breath and looking worried. The three men assumed it was a report from New POP1 since Public Channel 3 was the Media Center's cable broadcast from New POP1.

The men silently watched as News Drones fed one scene after another to the afternoon Cable News talking head. Shep Snider was trying to adlib as he viewed each new scene of destruction, fighting, fires, and mob violence.

Shep Snider usually made at least one dumb observation each day. His producer had given him a three-strike rule. If Shep said more than three stupid things in one broadcast, the producer would cut to Breaking News and give Shep the afternoon off, without pay.

Public Channel 3 had already called their evening reporters, but none were answering their phones. The three Public 3 News trucks and their crews were also missing. The News Drones had sent troubling pictures of cell phone G8 antenna assemblies being destroyed deliberately.

Shep normally full of dumb observations was speechless and this was a big problem for his producer. As Shep Snider stared at the pictures of a city of more than 10 million people losing all civil authority, a young 28-year-old reporter stood next to Shep.

"Hello, I'm Jessica Mannas. Thank you for watching our coverage this afternoon of these Breaking News developments." The women in the small room behind Jessica typed a streaming message across the bottom of the screen. "Breaking News Developments."

As you see from these Drone News Feeds, if you live in the areas of New POP1, New POP2 or New POP3 you should follow your Active Shooter training. Most of you should shelter in place."

"Aaaa, that is right Jessica. Anyone in New York or the surrounding areas should find cover and wait for the civil authority to establish peace among the populace…." Shep's sound mike was cut, and he looked over at his producer, shrugging as if to ask, "What did I do?"

Jessica Mannas took over the report as two men escorted Shep Snider from the building to never read the news again. He had offended many by calling their city New York. Reminding everyone of the riches of the corporate evildoers that had so blessed Old New York City.

Jessica continued, "Everyone watching this broadcast in New POP1 (she emphasized the correct name) should not expect emergency services to be available for at least 72 hours. We will try to get a statement from POP1's Fire Chief, Mike Flanders. I know that Denny's brother Mike will be able to put all our minds at rest regarding the present chaos."

Denny Flanders motioned for his assistant to turn the sound down, as he reached for his cell phone. "Hi Mike, where are you? Good, stay there and don't answer your phone." Most of the public did not know that Mike Flanders owned beachfront property close to Old Myrtle Beach.

Old Myrtle Beach had rejected its POP renaming by sending the *1st Quarter* Administration one message, "NO new POOP names." So, the Administration had no name for Old Myrtle Beach. It had been taken off all maps and all the other cities got the message. Accept your new non-offensive POP name or disappear from maps and official registries.

Denny's brother Mike Flanders was on a month-long vacation in Old Myrtle Beach. He had no Emergency Response Training. He had been given the job because of his brother. Denny knew he would just get in the way. No reason to send Mike to New POP1.

The three men continued to watch the large TV, without speaking. Until finally the broadcast feed stopped and was replaced by a one camera feed of an empty newsroom. Just before the feed was lost the Public Channel 3's Afternoon Newsroom seemed to be filling with smoke.

Raul was the first to speak. "I feel that as important as these meetings are, I should get back to the Media Center in Richmond. We have the capability to replace Public Channel 3's broadcast feed with encouraging news."

Denny nodded. Raul continued, "I will go along with any of your decisions about the vouchers and other matters of our dollar supply."

Raul moved slowly to his armored transport. He left his luggage to be delivered to his Richmond Residence later. As he drove down the long winding driveway, Raul reviewed his options, now that it looked like everything was falling apart.

Raul knew enough about business to realize he had just witnessed what businesses strive to avoid. When you are in business and you over promise and under deliver, your customers let you know by their reactions to your products.

The *1st Quarter* had been over-promising and under-delivering to its citizens for years. Raul knew that Government is one of the only Zero-Sum areas of life where there is no feedback loop. Are the citizen-customers happy? A normal business judges customer happiness by reports on sells and growth.

Denny's Administration had just got a feedback loop that they could not ignore. The loss of New POP1 was the beginning of the end of Denny Flanders's Administration. It may be the beginning of the end of the *1st Quarter*.

Raul's plans to be a part of the New United States' top leadership had failed, when Eric Swan detonated a bomb at the Bethany Assembly. He had reviewed the many restrictions on politicians in the new Bill of Rights and the new Constitution and decided that he was more suited to top-down management with minimal accountability.

Now he had to decide his next political steps. When the *1st Quarter* ran out of dollars what would the people do to exist in an uncertain financial atmosphere? Raul had a plan.

32

Escaping the *1ˢᵗ Quarter*

James looked confused. Hannah grabbed James's Go-bag and Janet grabbed 2 larger duffel bags. There were two older SUV's, dirty and dinted, in their garage. None of James's neighbors had seen these vehicles in James's upscale 4 car garage.

Tom jumped into one and Janet got into the other SUV driver's seat. Tom checked the glove compartment and saw James's old *Right to Pay* gun. Tom had personalized this car and reinforced the side panels and doors with Kevlar. Janet's car was similarly bulletproofed.

Both SUV's had had the gas tanks replaced with larger tanks and new suspension systems, so the vehicle looked normal as it drove down the road. They were much heavier than they looked.

Tom and Janet drove out of the gated community. They followed each other to the prearranged meeting place - Option Z's Western point.

It was 5 p.m. and Tom prayed that the rest of the Believers' group could get out of the city before dark. As Tom pulled up to the old country house on Old Mountain Road near the old Lebanon Reservoir, his prayers were answered.

As he pulled into the old metal building behind the house, Tom saw the 2 old and dirty station wagons and 2 old pickups with campers attached. One of the campers had the side-back window broken and repaired with heavy dark plastic tape. The other back windows were painted black except for a few missed areas. These areas were strategically placed for someone on the inside to lookout.

Tom had arranged for these 4 vehicles to also be bulletproofed and to have expanded gas tank capacities. He had also arranged for the campers to have modified tops that carried water and gas cans – now empty.

The group met in the old country house. All 6 vehicles were in the large rear metal garage and workshop. "We need to get past Pittsburgh to be safe. Once we get past Pittsburgh we will be in the New United States. There should be some form of border checks somewhere in or around Pittsburgh. I would like to detour around Old Pittsburg South to I70 if we can." Tom was talking fast.

"Once we are past the border checks and in the *2nd Quarter* – I mean the New United States, we are to make our way to Liberty IN. Take these old paper maps. Each of you take your copy in case we get separated. Do not use GPS. I assume you have already taken your cell phone batteries out." Tom looked around.

James looked a little guilty. "I'll do it right now, sorry."

The inside of the old country house just off Old Mountain Road was cramped with 29 adults, teens and children. One Believers Group member named Nicole had brought a couple that Tom did not know.

Tom nodded for Nicole to come into the back area of the house. "Who is this couple? And why did you bring them?"

Nicole a soft-spoken but strong-willed 20 something responded, "I couldn't leave them. They became believers last week and I was just going to – you know – start to teach them how evil the New Morality's actual practices are…"

"You shouldn't have brought them. There are thousands of Believers in New POP1. We are leaving because our assignments are over, and the city is falling apart. Tomorrow there may not be a New POP1 – or POP2 or POP3, for that matter."

Nicole, not showing any emotion, but obviously troubled said, "They did not know any other Believers. I couldn't abandon them."

"OK, ok but you have got to get them to allow us to search their things BEFORE we leave. And they have to give us their cell phones until we get to the New United States." As Tom finished with Nicole, he went into the large metal building behind the house and watched as the 5-gallon metal containers were filled with water.

"What are you doing?" Tom yelled at James, surprised at what he was seeing. James had cleaned the windows on two of the station wagons. Tom calmed himself down, "James, dump the water out of that bucket and go out back and get some dirt. Mix it with this oil." Tom pointed to a copper-colored can, "And smear it over every window of the vehicles you just cleaned. They are supposed to be dirty – on the outside."

James looked as if a light had gone on inside his head. "OK, I am sorry – I see now." Tom did not have to explain any further.

There were 50-gallon barrels of gasoline lining the back wall and Jim Brooks was using a hand pump to fill the vehicles and containers hidden on the top of the camper shells. Jim looked up and said, "If someone is above us, they will see these containers. But from the road, they will be well hidden."

Jim Brooks was one of the drivers and would lead one of the three groups of two vehicles each. Tom would lead another. Tom entered the cramped family room area and raised his voice loud enough for everyone to hear.

"EVERYONE, we need two drivers and one leader for the 2ⁿᵈ camper and station wagon group. I know James has volunteered but I need him with me. Anyone have ideas?"

Several people raised their hands to volunteer but most of the group looked over at David Micah, a lean young man in his early 30's as the man for the job. They had all heard about the close call with the school officials and David and Ana's daughter.

Tom looked at David and his wife and asked, "OK, can you drive the 2nd camper and take the lead if we are separated?"

David nodded and said, "Can I pick the person to drive the station wagon going with me?" Tom nodded and continued. "We should only use these walkie-talkies. When we are past Pittsburg, we can start using GPS and cell phones to communicate.

"If we get separated and one of you does not show up at the next Marked Meet on these maps, I will turn my cell phone on and the person who is lost or delayed will have to turn your cell phone on too.

"We will wait, but if you are delayed a long time, just keep going to the next meet. We will start with two groups of three vehicles a few minutes apart. But if we need to, we will break into three groups of two vehicles each. I don't know the range on these walkies, so let's keep as close as possible.

"We do not need to stop for gas, water or food. But we may be stopped, and we may have snippers firing at us. If that happens, radio with these 25-year-old walkies. Jim, please take some adults to the back building and we will train everyone on how to use these relics."

Raul Flies to Safety

Raul looked back at the large house surrounded by rolling green hills and strips of planned wooded areas and hoped he would never see this place again. He instructed his driver to take him to the old FCC building where the bottom floors were being used for a New Morality Training Center. Raul's 3 adult children worked there, compliments of having their father as one of the 3 Top Administrators.

Raul called his children's cell phones. "We have to go to an emergency meeting in the South. I will be flying out of AAFB and I need you to get your children and spouses and meet me there in 3 hours."

Raul's armored vehicle pulled up to the old FCC building and two armed guards jumped out. What used to be the Thomas Jefferson Memorial had been taken over by a group that wanted to be left alone.

Jefferson had been removed by the mobs years ago and stucco-covered any words on the interior of the Memorial. The expanse of stairs provided a defensible position to everyone in the enclosure. The guards kept their eyes on the water area in the general direction of the old Memorial.

Raul walked calmly into the New Morality Training Center and past the guards to his adult children's separate offices. He was adamant that they must come with him. He explained this building was being reassigned anyway and they should get their personal items and come with him now.

Raul's 43 relatives and 10 in-laws met at AAFB at 6 p.m. the afternoon that New POP1 fell into chaos. By 7 p.m. the airplane was in the air flying South toward 1POP 54 – old Columbus Georgia's Fort Benning.

Once Raul's plan to defect and be a part of the New United States fell apart because of Eric Swan and his DRAG Systems boss's bombs in Bethany, Raul had modified his escape plan.

As he sat in the large personalized airliner, he discussed with the adults the present condition of the *1st Quarter*. The kids, in the back of the jet, watched a New Morality Daytime Program hosted by a Philippine transsexual dressed in a miniskirt talking about sexual freedom.

Raul looked at the faces staring at him. Many of his relatives were accustomed to luxury and believed wholeheartedly in the *2 Commands of Love* and the *6 Principles of Behavior*. His three adult children could recite them from memory and they were considered leading teachers on the subjects.

> 1. Loving People means promoting Sexual Freedom and Tolerance toward all Sexual Behaviors.
> 2. Loving People means promoting Financial Justice and Equality for all men in every circumstance.

Now Raul was saving them from probable beatings, as the 1st *Quarter* Civil Authorities lost control. The New Morality Warriors had hurt so many unbelievers and heretics that Raul anticipated every New Morality Training Center to be attacked or worse.

Behind Raul's head, Denny Flanders's staccato voice boomed from the large screen on the front bulkhead. "Our Quarter … Will show the rest of the country … what it means to be fair … to everyone … We will not fail…

Raul looked over his shoulder and snarled, "Turn that damn thing off. He is so full of it.

"OK, I lied to you about the emergency meeting or whatever you told your families about this trip. New POP1 is no longer a safe place to visit. It looks like all civil authority has disappeared." He stopped to let this sink in. Everyone had been watching Channel 3's coverage of the riots before the newsroom went off the air.

"If you want to go back to Richmond, this plane will be returning immediately after we get off. You are all free to go back to your homes and hope for the best. I am relocating to the New United States. I have vehicles waiting for us in 1POP54 and the border is only a short distance from 1POP54."

Everyone looked confused and finally, Raul's oldest son asked, "Where is 1POP54?" He continued a little louder, "And what is going on?" He continued a little louder, "And what are you talking about?"

Raul's youngest son's name was Angel. And Angel had brought his father-in-law, Bob. Bob was Raul's age and spoke up, "POP54 is in Eastern Old Georgia – don't tell anyone I said Georgia, but sometimes you just don't know where something is without an old name.

Bob was on his third marriage. And his current wife had declined to come on this trip with Bob. This was a normal practice since they did not like one another and had to limit their time together.

Bob had a set of vices that had propelled him to top management at the Main Media Center in Richmond. Bob could spin a tail with only 2 facts. Many of the "news" stories coming from the Administration were actually Bob's stories. He should have been a fiction writer.

Raul shook his head in agreement. "Bob you must have been monitoring New POP1 from the Center. Were the Media Center managers anticipating today's riots?"

Bob thought and replied slowly to Raul. Raul was someone who could make or break a career. "We had no prior warning about today's riots. I was watching other feeds in the News Center and things are continuing to get very, very bad…"

Angel – a lowly editor in Bob's Media Center winced with Bob's hyperbole "prior warning." He thought, "What other type of warning was there?"

Raul interrupted Bob and addressed all the adults crowded into the front seats, "Denny Flanders is living in a fantasy reality. I was with him earlier today and when New POP1's riots started; he was more interested in who suggested the Disney Bear as the logo of the *Basic Necessity Stores*. He has sent a Richmond wide command to terminate whoever thought of the logo."

Bob interrupted Raul, politely, "I know who suggested the Bear. It was Randy Paris. He is an Ex-lawyer who can lie better than anyone I have ever seen…" This was a real compliment coming from Bob.

Raul continued, "Flanders should have been asking why anyone would name a store the *Basic Necessity Stores.* That is the worst name I have heard for a government voucher store. *Voucher Store* would have been better."

Bob broke in again, making Raul ask himself why he had invited Bob. Oh wait, he hadn't invited Bob, Angel's wife had… Bob blurted out, "It was the same guy, Randy Paris. Denny had just made a speech about people not having the Basic Necessities and Randy Paris suggested the new voucher stores should have that name – *Basic Necessities."*

Now Raul was sidetracked but really interested in the inner workings of this stupid process. "Did anyone connect the Disney Bear with the old song *The Bare Necessities*? The song was sung by a damn Disney Bear that looked a lot like the store logo."

Bob looked thoughtful, "I don't think anybody thought about that. We were all just trying to make points with Denny and Randy Paris got his kiss-up suggestions in before any of the rest of us."

Raul looked directly at Bob and said, "Be thankful you were slower than that other guy."

"Anyway," Raul raised his voice a little, just enough to get everyone's attention again. "I am leaving the *1ˢᵗ Quarter* and I am giving everyone on this plane the opportunity to leave with me."

Everyone was shocked and began to ask Raul why.

"BEFORE you ask – this flight is only 2 hours long, so let me continue. Since the New United States has brought the U.S. Dollar back under Federal control, the *1ˢᵗ Quarter* has been quickly running out of dollars. Denny Flanders has started a *1ˢᵗ Quarter* Voucher program to pay the workers that are working for the *Right to have a Job Initiative*. But there are not a lot of Disney Bear stores to take the vouchers.

"Private businesses are finding it hard to find capital and most banks no longer have branches open in the *1ˢᵗ Quarter* anyway. IN OTHER WORDS, in the next few months, there is a possibility that the *1ˢᵗ Quarter* may follow the North *4ᵗʰ Quarter* in becoming a land with no civil authority.

"To make things worse, the *1ˢᵗ Quarter* has confiscated and destroyed weapons for the last few years, under the *Fair Gun Safety Initiative*. The police and law enforcement have mostly quit and moved to the middle of the country. Emergency responders are no longer armed and hide if something bad is happening."

There was a long pause.

Bob who had become a reluctant spokesperson for the relatives asked, "What about the New Morality Warriors? They will keep the peace and enforce our laws. Right?"

Raul looked at Bob and then the rest of the group and they all started laughing. "Bob you have been writing too many of your 'stories.' Morality Warriors are activated and assigned to scare people into following our rules FROM the Media Centers and New Morality Training Centers. This is civil unrest on a citywide scale with EVERYONE calling emergency services at the same time.

"How many of you want to take the flight back to Richmond?" Raul said as he mockingly raised his hand. No hands went up.

"When this plane lands, I am changing my name, driving West and doing what I do best. I am going to be a politician in the New United States." With that Raul ended his little speech, sat down and reclined his seat as far as possible, banging into one of his relatives who quickly moved further back in the plane.

33

The Two Passages Out

Tom was crouched next to his SUV 100 miles into the 400-mile trip to safety talking on his cell phone. 4 vehicles were with him and David Micah's camper and station wagon were absent.

"So, you don't think there are any local authority drones patrolling the 202?" Tom stood up and relaxed slightly. Everyone had taken a bathroom break into the trees around them.

Tom continued, "Is the 422 guy where he is supposed to be?"

"OK, we will be coming toward you with 6 packages." Tom clicked his smartphone to hang up but left it on. He had been through this area on the back roads many times before, as he traveled between the *Quarters*. Now the local authorities were running on their own rules. Many local authorities were charging tolls to everyone on the road. Tolls were charged on a "how rich do you look" basis.

"We will wait here for David to catch up and then proceed to our next passage stop." Tom had worked out a 4-stop passage for any Believer Group trying to escape the persecution of the New Morality Warriors of the *1st Quarter*. The person called 202 had just given them the go-ahead to proceed to the second passage stop.

The group assembled under a large evergreen that looked like it might fall on them if the wind blew. Parents were feeding their children and several people formed a prayer circle. Tom as a lay pastor used to joke that the youth group always prayed without prodding when he took them on the steep back roads. Now praying for miracles and supernatural intervention was something everyone did every day, no prodding.

Tom thought, "Oh, for the days when we did not need daily miracles."

Jim Brooks was standing next to his SUV with a shotgun filled with Drone Buster shells watching the skies above. Jim's wife, Cindy had a hunting rifle propped up on the SUV and was using binoculars to scan the horizon. Jim's teenage daughter Dakota was watching a tablet that showed a live camera feed from a camera they had placed on the road they had just come down.

Dakota yelled out, "Here comes David Micah and the other car." Everyone started toward their vehicles. Jim Brooks yelled, "Everyone stay put. Drone incoming."

He fired his shotgun and the drone operator immediately took the drone straight up. David's camper and the other station wagon pulled into the clearing as a second shotgun blast took the drone down.

Tom yelled, "Everyone, let's get going – our next stop is marked with a "Y" on your maps if we get separated. Let's try to stay tight and keep together without rear-ending each other."

David's group did not have time to stop. Whoever was operating the drone knew that someone was on this road and the direction they were going. It was likely that the drone had been following the 2 vehicles bringing up the rear of their caravan.

All six vehicles accelerated quickly, in close formation. David Micah thought it was good that his camper had a bathroom.

10 minutes down the road at a major intersection, three beat-up jeeps sat in the middle of the road with armed men on each side. It looked like some type of homemade spike strips were placed between the jeeps.

Hannah sitting next to Tom was on the walkie talkie to Jim Brooks in the other SUV. "Jim, Tom says come up next to him. Everyone else stay back."

This was not local authorities. This was someone trying to rob them or worse. Tom and Jim's SUV's had reinforced front bumpers. Tom picked up the handset attached to a PA speaker mounted between his Fog Light Bar on the top of the SUV. "We can do this the easy way, or we can do this the hard way! You have one minute to move the center jeep and let us pass."

Hunting rifles appeared out of the left and right windows of each vehicle in Tom's caravan. A person climbed onto the top of David's camper shell, hidden by the false sides. The gas containers had been placed in the middle and the water containers had been placed on the outer perimeter two deep all the way around.

The vehicle's windows were muddy, thanks to James. Some windows were painted black and it was impossible to judge how many people or guns were in this caravan. The men standing on both sides of the road could count 4 long rifles on each side – 8 total. They could not see the two shotguns on the top of the campers.

After a tense 60 seconds, Tom revved his SUV and spoke into the handset, "Last chance – you ready for a gun battle?"

Three men moved quickly to drag the homemade spike strips and took off in different directions, driving the Jeeps over the shoulder of the road. The caravan slowly passed through the intersection, single file, watching for any other traps.

Hannah spoke into the walkie, "Jim, Tom wants you to hold back to the rear and watch for any other drones. If you spot one, we will stop, and you can shoot it down. We don't want to be followed.

Tom yelled into Hannah's walkie, "Hold on we are going to speed up." Night was approaching and Tom wanted to make the second passage stop before it was too dark.

Raul on The South Passage

Raul did not know that his caravan was traveling the approximate path in the South that Believers escaping persecution also took. He had picked this way because it seemed like the fastest way out of the *1ˢᵗ Quarter* and it was.

The New United States had established checkpoints 10 miles West of 1POP 54 - Old Columbus Georgia since Alabama was in the *2ⁿᵈ Quarter*. People using this passage out of the South *1ˢᵗ Quarter* were encouraged to leave by many politicians in the South *1ˢᵗ Quarter*. It had become a profitable business to confiscate assets from fleeing citizens on the South Passage.

1POP54 had a large assignment of well-paid New Morality Warriors. They were under orders to stop and take all assets from those leaving the *1ˢᵗ Quarter*. Large signs facing East were on both sides of all major roads leading West out of old Columbus.

The *FAIR CONFISCATION* Initiative
All personal property must be forfeited by
citizens leaving the *1ˢᵗ Quarter*.

This includes but is not limited to
automobiles, clothing, money, jewelry
or any other items deemed valuable.

Those with valid travel permits are excluded.

The *Fair Confiscation Initiative* was signed into law by Denny Flanders immediately following the last election. The election that was either a landslide victory for Denny or a grassroots rejection of Denny. It depended upon who you talked to.

Denny had explained that it was not fair for citizens to leave the 1st Quarter after experiencing all the benefits of living in the 1st Quarter, such as roads, water systems, electricity and cell phones. His position was that the property owned by the citizens of the 1st Quarter was not really their property since the 1st Quarter had given them so much.

The majority of those living in Richmond agreed – until they wanted to leave without a valid travel permit. Then they hid as many items as they could. The smuggling of dollars and family heirlooms was now more lucrative than smuggling drugs. Especially since most drugs could be purchased from the 1st Quarter Administration with competitive pricing.

Raul did not have to worry about the *Fair Confiscation Initiative* since he had a valid travel permit signed by - himself. Raul had brought 4 large footlockers full of large denomination U.S. Dollars and 6 duffel bags of miscellaneous high-value assets.

Since none of Raul's relatives had decided to go back to Richmond on the return flight, he had to obtain 10 more automobiles from the New Morality Warriors. That was no problem since part of Fort Benning was being used to house thousands of vehicles that had been confiscated under the *Fair Confiscation Initiative.*

Raul identified himself to the Supply Chain Manager – or whoever was in the office of the Supply Chain Manager since the Army no longer had a presence at Fort Benning. A large board hung on one wall. The board was full of keys – with row and number for each vehicle confiscated from westward-bound travelers. It was a rental car business where you didn't have to pay or show a credit card – no return necessary.

Raul's relatives excitedly went looking for their favorite vehicle and came back with row and number of the car they wanted. None of them picked with survival in mind. None of them thought that there would be a need for anything but luxury or comfort. None of them thought about the previous owner's loss of their personal vehicle.

Raul's large caravan left 1POP 54 traveling West with 14 vehicles of every model and size but all new and shiny. Everyone looked happy and in a good mood as they waved goodbye to the Morality Warriors in their masks and white jumpsuits.

Raul was in the front armored vehicle with his driver. The same driver that had left Denny's 550-acre estate. Raul had allowed his driver's wife and child to come with them. As his driver pulled out, into the wide highway, he thought, "Raul is so generous and kind." Raul agreed.

The Northern Passage – The Fourth Stop

Tom's main concern on this route was the checkpoints at bridges. Tom would explore detours later if this Northern Passage remained a viable escape route from the chaos in the 1st *Quarter*. His present route avoided the main Interstate corridors, now full of every type of vehicle imaginable.

Passage Stop Three's contact had warned them to avoid the checkpoints on their route on 209 and they had detoured North at Port Carbon.

This detour converged on I-81 for a short time in a forest in New Castle Township. Pedestrians and broken-down cars filled the main lanes going west as they used both sides of the interstate. The Believers caravan finally found the best Interstate Highway travel method going west was to use the eastbound outside shoulder. By maneuvering here, they could go off-road when the shoulder surface permitted.

It was on this 10-mile stretch of I-81 that everyone in the caravan sat in stunned silence, as they slowed to 5 MPH. The human tragedy, human cruelty and human frailty were displayed as families tried to escape the East Coast Population Centers.

Hannah keyed the walkie and Tom yelled, "Keep a close watch for weapons. I want each vehicle to have a long rifle stuck 10 inches out of a window. Keep close here."

David's wife, sitting directly behind him, holding a baby and the walkie keyed and David shouted, "How long are we going to be on the Interstate?" There was no answer.

Hannah spoke in a normal tone, "OK, everyone, let's all let our walkie operators speak softly and drivers tell them what to say. Going this speed, the people outside your vehicle can hear you, if you yell."

Hannah continued, "Tom wants each car to count how many seats are available. We will be reaching the Forth Stop. From there we have two hundred miles or less than a day if God helps us avoid bad stuff."

Each car full of Believers quickly responded with extra seat counts. Everyone's emotions were raw as they watched the human tragedy, they were passing. They were also aware of the highway criminals who were hiding behind broken down cars or roadside signs. Occasionally they had spotted someone lying up high on a billboard maintenance ledge with a rifle.

Tom held the walkie since he was stopped behind a newer model BMW fully stopped with no shoulder to pass. "OK guys, that is too large a number. I want a realistic count. The teens and kids can crowd together but adults cannot sit on each other's laps, even if you are married. We have too far still to go."

A slightly lower number came back. Tom shook his head, "OK, this is what we are going to do. Drivers you have to enforce seat counts. When you see someone who obviously needs help, click three times and we all stop. Offer the person a ride to the New United States. Identify yourself with the sign of the cross or if you have something to write on, draw a fish and use that."

The first group that was encountered in distress was 3 teenagers – 2 girls and one blond long-haired boy. They looked like they were 16 years old. They were surrounded by four men. Everyone had bats, poles or knives and it seemed like the perfect time to help.

Tom clicked three times and stopped. The driver's side back seat fired two quick shots into a close pine tree South of the Interstate. The four men scattered into the trees and Tom quickly rolled his window down. "We're Believers going to Old Pittsburgh. Do you want a ride?"

One of the teens wore a *2 Commands of Love* T-shirt. Hannah could see that they were fearful. She yelled out Tom's window, "See that camper two cars back? There are kids and teenagers in that camper. As Believers, we will not hurt you. We practice the 10 Commandments."

The teenagers looked even more confused since they had been taught that Believers were evil and cruel. As they glanced over their shoulders at the trees behind them, they quickly decided this nice lady looked safer than the road. They jumped into David's camper.

Once around the BMW, that looked like it was being driven by an eighty-year-old man that was sleeping, Jim Brooks camper clicked three times, and everyone stopped.

A man obviously bleeding and a woman with two children were crouched down behind a car full of personal items. They looked panicked, as they looked North to the Western lanes of the Interstate. The windows in their car were all broken.

Jim Brooks' wife, Cindy opened the front passenger door slightly and yelled, "We're Believers escaping to the 2nd *Quarter*. We can give you a ride." This family did not hesitate. Jim was positioned last in the caravan and was afraid that someone was shooting from the West Bound lanes at this couple.

Jim yelled out the front passenger door, "Go to the station wagon in front of us. They have a medical kit that might help." The family lugged four bags to the station wagon, while Cindy pointed a shotgun North, out her half-opened window. The bags wouldn't fit into the station wagon, so they dropped two and crowded into the station wagon. A teenager jumped out to help throw the bags on the top without securing them and ran back to Jim's SUV.

This rescue operation continued as the caravan slowly made its way to their Interstate Exit. James sitting in the front SUV behind Hannah was staring at the bodies lying along the grassy area between the Western bound and the Eastern bound lanes. "There are too many..."

Tom looked back at James, "We can't save the world, but we can save some." James nodded, with a resolute face. "James, if you want to help these people, next month I will be coordinating this Northern Passage with a number of Believers groups in New POP1." James nodded again. His face became even more serious.

The vehicles took in five more than their original vacant seat count. Using the beds in the campers as seats, they had taken in as many of the destitute travelers, as they could fit. Everyone was uncomfortable but feeling better about their ability to help a few of the neediest.

Once turning North to get back on their planned route, they had two more close calls with Local Authority drones. At 2 a.m. Tom's caravan pulled into the warehouse of Fairchild Unified (FU2) in Old Lewistown. The river was masking the sound of their vehicles.

The large warehouse doors closed, and everyone slowly loaded out of the 6 vehicles. Children ran first to the two warehouse bathrooms. Adults moved more slowly as they stretched. Tom's contact, Justin J. was wearing a holster with a firearm and watching the group from a distance.

Tom walked toward JJ – most people did not know JJ's full name - and motioned for him to turn his face away from the group. "There are strangers with us. We picked them up on the Interstate. I will watch the group and you should hide your face until we know their loyalties." JJ nodded and disappeared through a door that led up to a 2nd story set of offices.

The warehouse was empty, but someone had used multiple pieces of furniture and blankets to make 45 small privacy areas in the middle of the main warehouse floor area. Tom motioned to Jim. "Ask two watchers to go up there and watch." He pointed to windows twenty feet up.

"Take a couple of guys and talk with the newcomers. Make sure they know how important it is that their cell phones or other devices have the batteries taken out until tomorrow night when we enter the safety of the 2nd *Quarter*."

Tom continued, "David, please try to coordinate and help everyone find places to sleep and clean up. There are two more larger bathrooms through those double doors." Tom pointed to the front of the warehouse.

Tom raised his voice, "Let's keep the front lobby bathrooms Male and Female even though our visitors may not be accustomed to this male/female division. Right side female, left side male if the bathrooms are not marked."

Tom raised his voice even louder, "Listen, the Local Authorities can NOT be trusted. Do not call anyone. Do not go into the front lobby area where you might be seen from the street. We are LEAVING early tomorrow morning."

Early Next Morning

JJ was nervous. It was 9 a.m. and the vehicles would have to leave in daylight, for all to see. They would have to leave one at a time and meet outside of town.

Tom was in JJ's living quarters, but JJ still talked in a lower tone. "Once you get past Pittsburgh… You can go South to I-70 and I have been told that the new State of Northern Indiana is doing a good job keeping the westbound I-70 clear for motor vehicles. eastbound is being used for pedestrians and slower modes of transportation. You will even see horses and mule-drawn wagons…"

Tom responded, "What about the National Guard Border Patrols from the New United States?"

Justin J. shared what he had heard. "I have heard they are mainly busy on the I-90 Anti-American Wall since the rockets are continuing to be fired."

JJ was talking fast. "If - I mean WHEN you get to the I-70 and I-77 intersection, you will find a Welcome Center. It should have medical assistance. Somewhere around one of the abandoned Hotels – either Hampton or Holiday Inn."

Many hotels owned by Hilton had been abandoned and were now being used by those groups trying to help people flee the *1st Quarter*. Hilton had been promised one of three exclusive licenses to run hotels in the *1st Quarter*.

As most deals offered to large corporations from Socialist and Totalitarian governments, it looked like a great deal. But exclusivity only works when you are allowed to make a profit. Hilton had been forced into bankruptcy after *1st Quarter* regulations and fees were increased with price controls on their room rates.

JJ handed Tom a slip of paper, "Here is the last cell phone number I have for the Welcome Center at the intersection of I-70 and I-77. Tom shook JJ's hand and thanked him for risking his life for the cause. JJ watched as each vehicle left his warehouse area – 6 minutes apart.

34

Finding Safety and Freedom

Justin J. was right. Once past old Pittsburgh the group made it to the Welcome Center in 2 hours. I-70 West was open, and Tom's caravan was averaging 80 miles an hour. The new State of North Indiana's Highway Patrol armored vehicles were seen several times. They were equipped with large front bumpers and were quick to push disabled and abandoned vehicles off the roadway.

Almost immediately the group was encouraged by highway signs with highway rules. And the rules were being enforced. The whole atmosphere changed from oppressive fear and chaos to guarded hopefulness that comes from good men maintaining civil order.

The Speed Limit signs had been replaced with instructions for slower traffic. Most said:

**PEDESTRIANS
USE EASTBOUND LANES
ONLY**

Westbound lanes could go as fast as they wanted. Enforcing speed limits, when people were afraid of being shot or robbed was impossible and the new State of North Indiana was being run by pragmatic, one term businessmen and businesswomen. Rules were made with common sense and decades of intelligent decision-making experience.

Somewhere around Wheeling roadside billboards started announcing the Welcome / Help Centers with the number of miles left before you arrived. Many of these signs were hand-painted over existing billboards.

The Welcome Center

As Tom walked into the old Hampton Inn, now a Welcome Center according to the large sign in front, he recognized Joe Mack from Richmond. "When and how did you get here?" Tom was genuinely surprised and happy that his friend had escaped the *1st Quarter*.

Joe Mack looked past Tom, as he shook Tom's hand. Tom half hugged him, as Joe said, "There is a tent next door with medical help from a local Believers Group. You should get that guy help." Pointing to the man that they had rescued on the Interstate. The station wagon medic had been administering first aid, but the man was very pale.

Tom relayed the message to the group and 2 families, who needed medical attention immediately left.

Joe Mack returned Tom's half-hug and said, "At 11 tomorrow morning, we will have a Jobs and Housing Information Meeting in the larger conference room." He gestured to the left corridor. "You and your group should come."

Tom helped everyone as they checked into their rooms. The rooms were free, and meals were served in a conference room by the same Believers Group providing medical assistance. Tom suggested to everyone to get something to eat and relax in their rooms. Most had not had a shower for five days. Many of the group went directly to their rooms. Families were assigned connecting rooms.

As Tom stood to the side of the Lobby, he watched people slowly enter and start to read the information signs.

Free food to your right

11 a.m. Job and Housing Information Meeting to your left
Free Medical Help outside to your right
Welcome Center Help provided by North Indiana Believers
Jobs and Housing Help Provided by
Northeast Businessman's Coalition.

Tom watched the guards on the gas station's roof across the street. Tom had greeted three other guards as he entered the Welcome Center. This place was secure enough to be a place of peace. The idea of armed security that brings peace was foreign to the foolishness taught in the *1st Quarter*. Tom thought, "I have entered the land of the sane."

Many of the families who entered the lobby began to cry. Some women fell to their knees with emotional relief. Everyone entering was dirty and had varying degrees of emotional distress showing on their faces.

The Next Day

After showers and a good night's sleep on a bed with clean sheets, everyone in the group stumbled into the Believer's Free Meals conference room. A counter filled with breakfast foods and a refrigerator with juice and milk was at the back of the room. One armed guard stood at the entrance door. A reminder of continuing danger from some who might steal or kill.

Tom, David Micah, and John Brooks were still functioning as leaders for the group helping families navigate to get their breakfasts. Tom invited everyone to attend the 11 o'clock information meeting in Conference Room 4.

Joe Mack was at the front of the large Conference Room 4. There were tables around the sides of the room with names of different groups providing assistance to those fleeing the *1st Quarter*. In front of the room behind Joe Mack was three large overhead screens. Each screen was playing a series of information messages.

Each message began with the same wording.

This Welcome Center is NOT a Government Enterprise.
The New United States' Federal government
does not provide charity to any citizen.
This Welcome Center is NOT a State Government Enterprise.

The messages then continued with job descriptions, housing areas and other information that may help those who had lost everything to escape to freedom.

Each message ended with the same wording.

> *We encourage people to talk with the Transportation Centers and find your relatives in the New United States, before using the charity offered here.*

Tom arrived at 10 o'clock to talk with Joe Mack and find out as much information Joe might have about the Richmond area. But Joe was busy preparing his presentation, so Tom sat off to the side and waited.

As people slowly entered the room, they looked confused as they read the overhead projectors. Women and men were stationed behind the side tables to answer questions about their specific table's subject.

Most were confused by the mention of Believers and the concept of "no government help." People wondered through the room talking with those behind the information tables. They had not been exposed to religious charity or other forms of non-government help. Even when corporations helped the *1st Quarter* with partnerships, the credit was always given to Denny Flanders and his Administration.

Joe Mack tapped the mike several times to make sure it was on at 11:10. There were over 250 people in the room.

"We have a smaller group this morning. I welcome you to the New United States. We are happy you made it to freedom from the chaos and the restrictive policies of the *1st Quarter*." Joe Mack had lost weight since he and Tom had met in Richmond. But his head was still only a foot or so over the podium.

Tom thought, "A small group of over 250 people? How many people were arriving each day at this Center?"

Joe Mack continued speaking clearly, as a few babies began crying in the back. "I represent a group of businesses who want to see our Free Markets here – in the middle of the country succeed. There is no hidden agenda. This group of businesses knows that you need jobs that pay enough to house and feed your family. These business owners watched as the middle class of our Republic disappeared.

"The charity that you see here is from the Believers of North Indiana. They take donations from all Believers that want to give to the poor. They will help you with medical needs, temporary shelter and basic food. They will also help you travel to wherever you are going.

"I would like to ask the Believers sitting in front of me to consider donating one month of your time serving this Welcome Center if it fits into your plans. We need you. The 4th floor of this hotel has living quarters for you and your family if you stay. We are not asking for long term commitments – only one month."

Joe Mack continued with information details about the area and the jobs available further West. Then he stopped and looked over at Tom. "I would like to welcome and honor one of my good friends who has helped save many lives and has changed the course of our Nation." Joe reached out his hand toward Tom, "Tom would you like to address this group?"

Tom was used to addressing larger business groups. He got up slowly and took the mike from Joe. "I have crossed the passage you have just crossed many times. And I have lived over 80% of the time in the *1st Quarter* for the last 4 years.

"It took courage for you to come here. Now it will take courage to stand up for liberty and personal responsibility. As you travel West, you will find radical changes. It will be like exiting *The Twilight Zone* or arriving on a new planet."

There were grunts and chuckles since *The Twilight Zone* was one of the approved programs of the *1ˢᵗ Quarter*. Everyone quieted their babies as Tom continued.

"As you go west you will not experience the lawlessness that threatened your lives in the passage you just traversed. But you will not be able to sleep on the streets. City and county police officers – with guns – will enforce vagrancy laws, loitering laws AND trespassing laws.

"Joe Mack has told me there are classes tonight to orientate you to this new idea of Peace through Order because we respect one another. There are charitable shelters in each community, and you will be required to use them if you cannot take care of yourself.

"The government of the New United States is not here to feed, clothe or house you. It is here to maintain order. The will of the majority STOPS at the rights of the individual. So, you cannot pitch a tent on someone's back 40 acres. You will be arrested for trespassing.

"You will not be allowed to litter and make the rivers, forests and green areas your personal playground. You will need permits to use the campgrounds and no one is allowed to live in the campgrounds.

"You are entering a different country with different rules. I assume 99.99% of you did not come all this way to just replicate the chaos that you are escaping. I would be happy to talk with any of you, personally about the differences. You are leaving the freedom to live with little or no accountability that comes from Socialist thinking. No accountability is a lawless approach to living.

"Find your relatives, find a job and accept the charitable help that is being given to you here and in the communities of the New United States. Here you have only a few guaranteed rights.

"The right to be left alone -
"The right to have politicians held accountable -
"The right to pursue your own happiness -
"The right to be free -
"The right to have and succeed in your own life -
"The right to be protected from foreign and domestic threats"

The room sat in silence. The Believers in the room knew the truth of what Tom had just said. But most of the travelers in the room had spent their whole life in the *1st Quarter*. Most seemed excited and a little scared at the new opportunities and the new uncertainty.

In the *1st Quarter*, they had been told what to think and what to say. They had been slowly beaten into submission by the Media Centers and the cultural pressure to submit or be punished. Now they were being set free and they were not sure they wanted to be completely free. Maybe a little freedom would be good. But complete freedom, meant full responsibility for their own actions and failures.

Joe Mack looked at Tom and then looked at the room. "Thank you, Tom, let's get together and talk about old times, fake elections and the fall of New York. You were there and I am sure it was scary." A few gasps went up from the group when Joe Mack uttered the forbidden name – New York.

One Week Later

Tom was saying goodbye to the group. David Micah was taking his family in one of the station wagons with several friends to Central Iowa where he had relatives.

The campers and SUV's were assigned for another mission East to rescue more persecuted Believers and others who may need help crossing.

Jim Brooks, his wife, and daughter were all sad to see the group break up. They were volunteering for one month at the Welcome Center. Tom had asked them to come south, after their month of service was up. There would be more Welcome Centers needed and Charter Bank had Corporate offices two hours south.

The teenagers they picked up on the Interstate had decided to go North, even though everyone had told them that rockets were still being shot across the Anti-American wall between the two Great Lakes. They had relatives in Old Detroit. Everyone hoped they would be stopped by the wall.

The man who had been injured on the Interstate decided to become a Believer and help for one month with Jim Brooks at the Welcome Center. He was happy every day, knowing that he and his family could have easily been murdered. In the past, he would have called their being saved a random act. Now he called it God's love and plan for his life. Whether random or Divine, He would thank God each day.

The New POP1 group of Believers each made their own choice. Some decided to help the Northeast Businessman's Coalition by providing transportation for those wanting to try a job further West. These jobs were well paying and escaping from the *1st Quarter* had left their families destitute.

James's *Right to have a Job Initiative* allowed Tom to create good relationships with many men and women who wanted to help the New United States succeed with free markets. Motivated by self-preservation these businessmen had taken quick steps to save their families and parts of their businesses. All those Tom had warned had taken steps to move their businesses to the New United States quickly.

Several of the group were accompanying Tom, Hannah, James, and Janet further south to establish a new group called *Businessmen of America*. Tom would also support the creation of more Welcome Centers along the *1st Quarter's* Western Border.

35

Dedicating the New United States

6 Months Later

It had been 6 months since New POP1 fell into lawlessness. The electricity had been out in most of the city for several months and attempts to report on New POP1's condition had been delayed by the inability to travel in or out of the city without being attacked.

The day New POP1 ceased to exist as a city was first labeled *Connor's Division Day* by Richmond's Main Media Centers. Now it was called *Connor's D Day*. Thousands were escaping the chaos through the Northern Passage as people realized they could not depend upon the *1st Quarter* Administration to help them.

Richards, the Ex-Californian and 65 other leaders of Believer Groups, Liberty Groups and Political Groups of the New United States were meeting in a casino north of Oklahoma City.

The Native American Reservations, which were renamed *Original Lands* were not celebrating the current political changes, since their governmental structure had never reflected the freedom of the old Republic.

The *Original Lands* and its occupants were still mainly totalitarian in their top-down social structure. Property ownership was limited to a few very rich individuals called Elders. Everyone supposedly owned the land. But in practical terms when everyone owns something, no one owns it. A small group of rich people "controlled" the *Original Lands*.

The *Original Lands* leaders were keeping their heads down, hoping that the New Federal Government would honor the lack of human rights that the old United States had instituted and even helped maintain in the *Original Lands*. Those who were not rich had given up any hope of upper mobility in the corrupt power structures.

Richards's large group had had no problem booking a July 4th Party under a fictitious name at Star River Casino. July 4th Celebrations had been outlawed as insensitive by Judicial Rulings. The old Federal Courts' purges were commonplace because it only took a small group of angry individuals to get a new restrictive mandate.

The *July 4th* Purity Purges had not yet been rescinded. Now that liberty was being guaranteed by the new Constitution most Purity Laws were expected to be deemed unconstitutional. Striking down laws and court-ordered mandates was one of the only powers the new Federal Court had been given by the new Constitution.

Many knowledgeable observers blamed the Federal Court's tyranny as one of the main causes of the disintegration of the old Republic. The old courts had forced all other institutions in the nation to submit to its will as if it had been given a dictator's power. The new Constitution now limited the Federal Court's powers significantly.

The Meeting

Ja'Ron Stuart and Craig Carmichael called the meeting of this select group to order. Ja'Ron started, "This Casino reminds me of the many times my father Stuart and I would take a day and drive out of the LA Area…."

Ja'Ron continued, "Thank you for coming. This is NOT a government meeting. You have been invited to participate because you are a leader of a group that represents at least 50,000 people. Not everyone who was invited has responded and so if you are looking for a friend, they may or may not be coming."

Dedicating the New United States

Craig Carmichael sitting at a long table at the front of the large room spoke into the mike in front of him. The four surround sound speakers boomed out, "Yes we are happy to meet you and hope to talk with you all personally about our New United States.

"All participation in this meeting is voluntary. This could be a sensitive subject for some, and we understand if you become uncomfortable."

President Richards sitting to the right of Craig and Ja'Ron spoke. "We are here to talk about dedicating our New United States to God and asking for God's help as we go forward. We know some of you are not Believers and if for any reason you are uncomfortable with our discussions, please feel free to express your feelings. We will be respectfully and hear all points of view."

The group of leaders looked at one another and spoke softly back and forth. Richards then continued. "Please call me Terry Richards, Rick Richards, Terrance Richards or just Richards. But do not call me President Richards. I do not ask this because I disagree with the final decision of the Bethany Assembly, to have a Federal President.

"I ask this because our new nation needs a time of reflection that looks to its leaders as servants and not kings. The label of *President* has been and still is a title that was misused in the former Republic. Please help our citizens learn a new way of living and viewing politicians. And especially a new expectation or may I say, definition of a President."

Ja'Ron addressed the full group. "You may not know this, but my father was an elder in a small Believers group in SoCal. The church he helped is now beachfront property if anyone actually wanted to live there. We have invited people with varying opinions to be on our panel. Should we Dedicate to God of our new Nation? Here are our panelists."

"Connor Quinton – yes the real Connor Quinton of Connor's D Day. He is a Conservative Jew and brings his unique insight." A thirty-something man stood at the left end of the table and bowed.

"Jessica Manas – yes the women who watched Shep Snider meltdown on Channel 3, as New York crumbled. Jessica is an anti-religion Conservative that only recently made it out of the *1ˢᵗ Quarter*." A girl that looked no older than 23 stood at the far right of the panelist table. She was dressed - business casual. She smiled and sat down.

"And finally, Clark Williamson's wife Lisa - she has come to speak for her late husband. I know we all miss Clark and have been praying for his family." A Sandra Bullock look-a-like was sitting next to Richards. She smiled, stood, nodded and sat back down.

Some of the 65 leaders had been thinking about gracefully going to the bathroom and not coming back, once they had heard the reason for this gathering. But now everyone was looking forward to hearing what these true celebrities – in this post-celebrity age was about to say.

Craig Carmichael took the lead. "We are going to express our personal opinions about religion and how our leadership can either help our nation or hinder it. If you have a comment or an opinion, please write it on the slips of paper in front of you. We have time to explore everyone's ideas and hear everyone's comments."

All the leaders had narrow tables in front of their chairs. No one had been assigned seating. Craig had expected everyone to just choose a seat that they were comfortable with. The room had filled up from the middle to the back and now several people moved up to the front row vacancies.

Ja'Ron spoke, "We would like Lisa to speak first." He turned to her and said, "We honor you and your husband's service to the New United States. We were all devastated by Clark's murder at the Bethany Assembly."

Dedicating the New United States

Lisa Williamson was 5 foot 10 and had piercing dark eyes. She had a relaxed smile that came from spending much of her life being Mrs. Clark Williamson. There was a genuineness about her that made people want to be her friend.

"You all know what my husband's political positions were. I am here to talk about our religious beliefs. Clark was what we use to call a Pro-Life Catholic before those terms were banned and all Christians went underground and became Believers."

Lisa took a drink from the glass of water in front of her and continued, "I assume most of you could have guessed Clark's religion as Conservative. He was always surprised by his liberal well-educated friends when they acted as if Christianity in America was something to fear.

"He believed, as the Founding Fathers believed, that Democracy cannot succeed without a culture that teaches our citizens to live with respect for their fellowman. Clark felt and I still feel that the Ten Commandments is the basic guide to what that respect should look like." Lisa sat down. She was obviously not in love with the sound of her own voice and smart enough to condense her remarks to the basics.

"Thank you, Lisa," Craig caught by surprise at the shortness of her comments, jumped up and said, "Next we would like to ask Jessica Manas to speak."

Jessica remained seated and did not lean forward, as a trained Talking Head learns to do. "No one in the *1ˢᵗ Quarter* knew my parents were conservative. They taught me that the New Morality was really evil and disrespected everyone who did not agree with one political point of view.

"So, I have grown up with a unique view of religion and politics. I have always been anti-religion. Anti-religion in the sense that we should all just believe what we want to believe and not bring our beliefs into the public square.

"This includes Anti-American religions and anti-New Morality and," looking toward Connor Quinton, "Anti-Jewish religion. I do not believe in God. I would like to believe, but I just don't.

"I will try to have an open mind and listen to what you all have to say. I believe I represent many of my younger generation that would like to understand something other than tyranny. We are tired of the deceptions that change the meaning of words from one day to the next.

"Now for the good stuff. What did Shep look like when Connor broke Old New York? I will be happy to talk about *Connor's D Day* and the panic and the stupidity that surrounded me on Channel 3 and later in the Media Centers. We were evacuated to a New POP2 Media Center when our building caught on fire. The Emergency Responders were stopped, by rioters from putting out the fires on our building and the whole block burned to the ground."

There was nervous laughter and a few, "I want to hear about that." Scattered throughout the room.

Craig looked to Connor and Connor stood up and moved around in front of the panelist's table. It seemed Connor loved talking with people about serious subjects. He showed the confidence that someone who has thought through his ideas for many years.

Connor was smartly dressed, lean with a friendly smile. "I will not be arguing with anyone today or later tonight. It is my goal to bring clarity to our positions. And I hope I am remembered for my ideas and not the fact that the *Connor Quin Daily* was one of the factors that broke the power of the *1st Quarter* Administration.

"We might want to remember that the *1st Quarter* Administration created a perfect storm, by disarming good people and discouraging Law Enforcement. Then running out of money, food, and jobs.

"That leads me to my first point. Yes, I am a conservative Jew, but I am also a citizen of this country and we need to decide what government's relationship should be to religion. Should the government be our Moral Teacher?

"I would simply ask you to answer one question. I would really like to hear your response. What set of moral rules should we encourage our citizens to follow? That is the question. Should we use the 10 Commandments and the Golden Rule? Or should we all get together and come up with a new set of moral rules?

"Could we be humble enough to accept that thousands of years of human relationships have been affected by one book – The Book. There is only one set of rules that comes from ancient Christianity and Judaism. Or do we think that we are smart enough to start all over again and come up with something new?

"I think we all know that our Government's moral education will not bring order to such a large and diverse nation like ours. There are people, in the 1st and 4th Quarters contacting me. They are looking for a way that their areas might become a part of our New United States. They are looking for answers.

"I would present this to you. Our decisions today, may be more important than the First Congressional Assembly that is happening in a few months. When we meet as Federal Lawmakers, we can make mistakes and then correct them. But when it comes to honoring God, we either honor God or we don't honor Him.

"To you Jessica and to all the Jessicas that we might meet in the years ahead, I would ask you to consider honoring the principles that I believe God instituted thousands of years ago. I would ask you to consider encouraging all human beings to follow Judeo-Christian behavior toward one another.

"Jessica, in this acceptance of the actions that citizens are encouraged to follow by Judeo- Christian religion you will need to take a thoughtful approach. You may have to separate the rituals from the moral rules. You may have to think through your own feelings toward a God that you have been told is unloving and only wants to take all the fun out of life.

"To all of you who CANNOT believe in God, to all you who do not believe, I ask, "What moral code do you want to encourage when asking citizens to be good citizens?

"Finally, I would ask – do we want to have a country where each person is free to believe and practice his own beliefs publicly without retaliation from the haters;
without retaliation from the bullies;
without retaliation from those who would try to force us to act like they want us to act?"

Connor had been walking back and forth as he spoke, talking directly to the men and women in the room. The room broke into applause as many also believed as Connor believed. They believed that the New United States needed God's help. This nation would not last without people who honored God.

As the applause died down, the Ex-Californian picked up the mike in front of him and stood. "We need good citizens, or we will not have a good country. Citizenship classes, like the ones that were banned decades ago, may be a smart start. But what values do we base them on? A new moral code? I think we have seen where that goes."

Craig Carmichael stood and asked for people to put their comments in the baskets on their tables. After a 45-minute break, the room would reassemble and discuss the different views expressed.

The Next Day

After hours of discussion and statements from these men who represented large groups across the country, three groups emerged.

1. The No Government group
2. The Restricted Government group
3. The Pro-Government group

1 - The No Government group wanted no moral training of any kind initiated or developed by government. They wanted all civil laws to be based on the Book's principles but the government to stay out of all moral training.

2 - The Restricted Government group wanted government to allow groups the right to teach citizenship classes in government facilities using Judeo-Christian principles.

3 - The Pro-Government group wanted to depend upon government education and to avoid all religious influence. This small group who had roots in the 2nd and 3rd Quarter Administrations took the position that "they could do it better this time." Their arguments were that if only more money, more time and more resources were devoted to moral training the government could train people to be good since people were naturally good anyway.

Going forward there were no decisions made from this gathering. After three days, Connor Quinton closed the gathering.

"I am so thankful I had the opportunity to meet many of you. I know most of us have more clarity on these issues. We will have to do this again. As we close these meetings, I would like to lead us in a prayer. This prayer is from my heart to God's heart. If you agree with me, you may say Amen."

"God, we ask you to help us as we lead our new Nation.
"God, we ask that you direct us and keep your hand upon us.
"God, we pray that our Nation would be dedicated to right actions and blind justice."

Craig Carmichael, Ja'Ron Stuart, the Ex-Californian, Richards and 95% of the room stood. Jessica Manas, a seeming hold-out slowly stood with a sober look on her face.

Those standing said, "Amen." Some shouted and others said it quietly but all with sober and serious expressions spontaneously said it again.

"Amen."

36

Two Years and Counting

The 2nd Congress of the New United States was meeting on August first, location to be announced. It had been two full years since the new Federal Government had been elected in the *2nd Quarter and 3rd Quarter.*

Erick Swan was in the Anti-American Territories. He stood on the makeshift tower looking into the New United States. He was on a mission to listen and report back from the Congressional meetings to DRAG Systems.

DRAG Systems now monitored and would soon control the economy of 180 countries of the 202 presently registered with the United World Oversight and they were not happy. There were Liberty Groups trying to form Republics in several former Democracies.

DRAG Systems must fight nations that would try to enforce their sovereignty if they were to succeed in their Mission Statement – *To Serve and Monitor the Whole Earth.*

Erick squinted, as he looked into the distant *Lawless Lands* of Old Chicago that he was about to navigate. His trip would be mostly at night.

He looked down on the blackened and burned missile launchers below him still aimed to fire over the wall into the New United States. It was said by those in the Anti-America lands, "The safest place was next to a bombed-out Launch Site." U.S. Army deployments had started shooting back and they used high tech drones.

Erick climbed down from the tower to enter the tunnel that would lead him into this new Nation. It was almost dark.

Connor Quinton in Bethany

Connor Quinton had accepted a two-year assignment from Richards as Ambassador to the 1st Quarter and 4th Quarter. He was talking via secure military video links to many former officials in Florida and Georgia. He and many others had reverted to the old names of States, Cities, and Communities.

Connor had continued his Quin Daily News in the 1st Quarter and he was talking with a West Coast Liberty Group about expanding to the 4th Quarter. He regularly used the hardened communications network available in Bethany. Bethany had also kept heavy security and became a favorite location for Government meetings.

As Ambassador, Connor's job was to talk with those wanting to become a new State of the United States. He would explain how they could apply and then move toward legitimate elections and establish a new State Constitution. He explained to each group that the New United States Constitution had given the old States a 10-year period to follow 5 steps and apply to become a State.

The boundaries could be redrawn using common sense and political alignments. The New States must have the backing of a vast majority of its citizens to apply for New Statehood. Connor helped coordinate electronic Quin Daily News to these groups seeking freedom.

Raul and His Family

Raul and his family settled in Shreveport Louisiana. Their trip was uneventful since civil authority had been maintained in the Southern 2nd and 3rd Quarters.

His stash of cash and newer vehicles were a great help in quickly finding freedom in Free Markets. When Raul first escaped, his cell phone had rung every two minutes. But now it was assumed he had been kidnapped or killed in the chaos of the 1st Quarter.

Raul was very interested in becoming active in local politics. His old contacts with DRAG Systems had given him a few names of shady characters laying low in the middle of the country. Since DRAG Systems had been outlawed by the first act of the new Congress, Raul was waiting. He had bought a small mansion outside of town, only a few miles from the Texas border.

Raul and his family were slowly adapting to their new political environment. They were still Socialists and felt that they should have special privileges. They continued to break the law and mistreat their fellow man as they had done in the *1ˢᵗ Quarter*. Raul had become known as *The Bad Guy* who lived on the hill. The Southerners were much harder to fool than the well-educated of Richmond.

James and Janet at the Welcome Center

James and Janet were processing over 1,000 newcomers a day at the Elk River Welcome Center. They managed the 2ⁿᵈ largest Center in the country. As more businesses left the central *1ˢᵗ Quarter* for the free markets of a free Nation, more families followed them.

James and Janet were happy. They were happy to not have to fear for their lives each day. They were happy that they were doing what was right and helping people. James and Janet lived their beliefs and enjoyed doing it.

Denny Flanders in Richmond

Denny sat alone in one of his many offices in the Main Media Center of Richmond. Gordon and Raul had not been seen for months. Civil authorities had lost all control of the national mall and the surrounding area.

Denny had big ideas for a centralized and fully controlled economy. His economic ideas about saving money by not having the many expenses of Capitalism's competition had not worked out.

Business expenses, advertising expenses, billing expenses, and branding expenses were eliminated when there was only a few Administration Licensed Business. Denny's problem had been that all these activities (advertising, billing, and branding) were also business activities that had given someone a job and made someone else a profit.

But the biggest reason Denny's big ideas had hit a brick wall was the Capital of the Capitalist System he despised moved out of the *1st Quarter.* Six months ago, he had started printing *1st Quarter* Dollars that were soon deemed *Denny Dollars,* by the general public.

As Denny sat in his big office looking out at the empty Media Center parking lot, he was happy to think about all his programs and how they had helped people. He thought to himself, "If only more people had believed, if only we had had more money, if only we had had more time, I am sure that we could have made Socialism work this time."

All the Administration's initiatives were still functioning in Richmond, where the government employed most of the populace. But everywhere else people may have had the right to food, clothing, housing, healthcare, and a good retirement, but it was up to them to find it. The *1st Quarter* Administration had no money except *Denny Dollars.*

David Micah and Family

After saying goodbye to the New York Believers group David and his wife and kids settled in Central Iowa. They were fixing up an old farmhouse. David and Ana had started *Young Believers for Freedom.*

He and his family traveled from school to school and from church to church talking with School Principles and Believer Pastors about including their Civics Training in educational curriculums.

They were happy to raise their family far away from the chaos of the 1st *Quarter's* tyranny and lawlessness. They felt that it was their personal mission to help avoid the present world's deceptions by teaching the next generation about civic duty and free-market economies.

Richards and the Ex-Californian

Richards, Craig Carmichael, Ja'Ron Steward, and the Ex-Californian were finalizing the agenda for the upcoming Congressional meetings. The meetings were being held symbolically close to Independence Missouri. Each congressman and representative had submitted their requests for debate, discussion or laws they would like to explore passing.

Since the Congressional Sessions would only be 6 weeks long and then adjourn for 60 days, before reconvening in a different location, the Congressional agenda had to be coordinated before the meetings began.

The process of this coordination had not been determined, except for the First Vote of each session would be a vote to continue with either a modified or adopted Agenda. This Agenda had all the items previously submitted in a specific order that once First Vote was made, would be used for the session.

These Congressional Sessions were time limited by the new Constitution. If Congress could not agree with supermajorities on most items, no law would be passed.

As the men talked about the concerns now being submitted by representatives across the country, they took a deep breath. They had been fighting so long to see liberty re-established that they now slowed just enough to consider their successes and the responsibility that they presently carried.

Tom's Businessmen of America

Tom had finally settled down and married Hannah. Everyone in the group had been praying and hoping that the two would get together. But in times of chaos, personal happiness is put off to another time.

Tom and Hannah continued to travel from Welcome Center to Welcome Center coordinating Charter Bank's funds being provided to the businesses helping the Centers.

Tom's *Businessmen of America* had chapters in each of the 34 States, and he was busy traveling to promote free markets through responsible business practices. Tom had first wanted to name his organization *Believer's Businessmen of America* since his groups used the Book's moral principles as a guide. But he and Hannah had decided that they wanted as many businessmen in the group as possible as long as they believed in the same Ten Commandment Morality of free markets.

Tom and Hannah were happy living free. As they pursued their own happiness, they did what was right and continued doing good.

Wise Quotes

"When the people find that they can vote themselves money, that will herald the end of the Republic."
Sometimes attributed to Benjamin Franklin

"There is a reason why in New York Harbor we have the Statue of Liberty, not the Statue of Equality."
Charles Krauthammer from https://www.inspiringquotes.us

"Our Constitution was made only for a moral and religious people. It is wholly inadequate to the government of any other kind."
John Adams fromwww.brainyquote.com/quotes

"Of all tyrannies, a tyranny sincerely exercised for the good of its victims may be the most oppressive."
C.S. Lewis from God in the Dock: Essays on Theology (Making of Modern Theology)

"Indeed, a major source of objection to a free economy is precisely that it... gives people what they want instead of what a particular group thinks they ought to want.

Underlying most arguments against the free market is a lack of belief in freedom itself."
Milton Friedman from Capitalism & Freedom (1962)

"Sometimes I wonder whether the world is being run by smart people who are putting us on or by imbeciles who really mean it."
Attributed to Mark Twain

"Those that can give up essential liberty to gain a little temporary safety deserve neither liberty nor safety."
Benjamin Franklin from Objections to Barclay's Draft Articles of February 16, 1775

"Socialism, in general, has a record of failure so blatant that only an intellectual could ignore or evade it."
Thomas Sowell from The Thomas Sowell Reader

"Our unalterable resolution should be to be free."
Sam Adams from "The life and public services of Samuel Adams…"

"The moment the idea is admitted into society that property is not as sacred as the laws of God and that there is not a force of law and public justice to protect it, anarchy and tyranny commence."
John Adams from Defence (sic) of the Constitutions of the Government of the United States

"Our liberty cannot be guarded but by the freedom of the press, nor that be limited without danger of losing it."
Thomas Jefferson to John Jay, 1786.

"A Government of Laws, and not of men."
John Adams from Massachusetts Constitution, Bill of Rights, article 30 (1780) Works, vol. 4, p. 230

"If all printers were determined not to print anything till they were sure it would offend nobody, there would be very little printed"
Benjamin Franklin from Historical Review of Pennsylvania (1759)

"The natural progress of things is for liberty to yield, and government to gain ground."
Thomas Jefferson from Letter to Edward Carrington

"The powers delegated by the proposed Constitution to the federal government are few and defined. Those which are to remain in the State governments are numerous and indefinite."
James Madison from Federalist Papers

"Facts are not liberals' strong suit. Rhetoric is."
Thomas Sowell from Statistics and facts vs. rhetoric

"Here is my Creed. I believe in one God, Creator of the Universe. That he governs the World by his Providence. That he ought to be worshiped. That the most acceptable Service we can render him, is doing good to his other Children.

That the Soul of Man is immortal, and will be treated with Justice in another life, respect[ing] its Conduct in this. These I take to be fundamental Principles of all sound Religion, and I regard them as you do, in whatever Sect I meet them."
Benjamin Franklin from The Papers of Benjamin Franklin, Complete Set: Volumes 1-37

About the Author

Gregory B. Grinstead was the senior pastor of Palmdale Christian Fellowship, a church in Southern California for over 25 years.

Gregory and his wife Michelle have four adult children and four grandchildren.

Gregory is also the author of the following books.

Is God a Capitalist?
God's Perspective on Governments and Economic Systems

The Hidden Promise
Honoring Your Parents

God's Help for Parents with Adult Children
Hope and Healing for Extended Family Relationships

The Divided Church
How Christians Will Get the World's Attention Again

You can email the author at Greg@GregoryGrinstead.com.
Your opinions and insight are always welcomed by the author.

Go to www.GregoryGrinstead.com to order any of Greg's articles or books.

Made in the USA
Monee, IL
28 December 2019